WHERE GOOD GIRLS GO TO DIE

HOLLY RENEE

Where Good Girls Go to Die

Visit my website at www.authorhollyrenee.com.

This is a work of fiction. Names, places, characters, and incidents are the product of the author's imagination and are used fictitiously.

Cover Design: Regina Wamba
Editing: Ellie McLove
Drawing: Dustin Collins of Passion Fish Tattoo and Piercing Studio

Stay notified of new releases, sales, and monthly newsletters:
Join the Mailing List

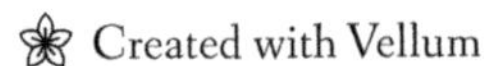

TO MY MOMMA

You've taught me that I didn't always have to be the good girl.

You've showed me that it was okay to be wild, funny, and rebellious.

You've pushed me to be bold and ambitious.

I've watched you dance like you don't give a damn who's watching and belly laugh with a carefree spirit that's infectious.

And I fell in love with everything that you are, and as a result, I learned to fall in love with myself.

So here's to you.

The woman who has always been the life of the party.

This one's for you.

CHAPTER 1

GIRLS, GIRLS, GIRLS

LIV

THERE COMES a time in everyone's life when they realize that the things they thought they wanted are never going to happen. All those dreams of happily ever afters and white picket fences, they disappeared through my grasp as if I was trying to hold onto a cloud of smoke. Useless and unrealistic.

I learned the hard way that reality was a cold, hard bitch. She didn't ease me into it slowly. There was no gentle push that had me blinking open my caramel colored eyes until I saw the truth in front of me.

I cliff dived.

Falling hard, frantically clinging to what I desperately wanted, I hit reality as if I jumped head first into a body of ice-cold water. Gasping for breath, the pain was instant, but unlike the water, it didn't make me numb. Instead, I felt that pain every day. It had settled into my bones causing a constant, dull ache.

My pain was as much a part of me as anything else. It was real and tangible, and just when I thought the pressure on my chest was easing a bit and I finally took a deep breath, reality reminded me who ruled and crushed me again just as easily as the first time.

I never expected that I would end up here. When I think back, I'm not really sure how it happened. Where everything went wrong.

It was a day just like any other. The smell of smoke and overly sweet perfume clung to my skin as I walked in the door. With the click of the latch, the world outside disappeared and I entered a world of mystery, lust and skin.

My steps were calculated and confident as I made my way over to my station, but my hands shook as I began rimming my eyes in coal black. It was easy to fool everyone else, too easy, but fooling myself was impossible. I searched my reflection for a trace of the innocence that once lay there. But all traces of the girl I used to know were gone.

Delicate black lace encased my breasts, a sharp contrast against my pale skin, and it would have looked beautiful if men weren't going to be yelling at me to take it off within the next few minutes. In a different situation, in a different life, I probably would have liked the feel of the soft fabric against my skin, but in this life, it was suffocating. It was a gentle reminder of what I had become, and it burned my skin like a brand.

I watched all the girls in the room as they put on their facade. Each one of them had a different story that led them here. It wasn't a choice many people made without reason. I'd be lying if I said I didn't know what brought me to this point, but fuck, I hated thinking about it. Not because my story was one of tragedy, but it was one of heartbreak. I let a man destroy me, and as a result, I became a coward.

"Liv, you're up doll," Mark called from the silk curtain before smiling at me.

Mark was sleazy, but he was nice to me. I bought his kindness by making him the most money, but I'd take it either way. I had no friends in Atlanta. I had no family. They were all back in Tennessee, but I couldn't think about Tennessee because it made me think of him. I couldn't afford to think about him. It fucked with my head. It fucked with everything.

I could feel the stares and hear the harsh whispers from the other girls as I walked by, but I didn't care about their opinions of me. There was a time when I would have cared what they thought, but that was long gone. All that mattered now was that the men loved me, no one here was close enough to hurt me, and I would leave with a wad full of cash at the end of the night.

"We've got a bachelor party in room one," Mark read from his clipboard in front of him. "They've paid a lot of money, and I promised them our best." He ran his chubby finger down my cheek, and I forced myself not to pull away from his touch. The smell of liquor and cheap aftershave choked me, but I hid my rush of nausea behind a fake smile that I had learned to master over the last few years. "You'll start, then I'll have some of the other girls join you."

Bachelor parties were one of my least favorite parts of this job. Tainted wasn't some hole in the wall club where just anyone could walk in. It was elite and the men who walked through those doors were as well. They had expectations. They had specific tastes, and Tainted catered to those tastes.

But bachelor parties?

They were another beast.

Men at bachelor parties were rowdy. Alcohol flowed, inhibitions were low, and the men were fueled by the idea of only being with one woman for the rest of their lives.

I took a deep breath as I made my way to room one. Several men sat in the private room facing the stage where I would dance. Their eyes searched the black curtains waiting for me to appear as the lights in the room began to dim. Seduction was in the air, and I was the temptress.

The strong beat of the music shook the stage below my feet as I got settled behind the curtain. My hands gripped the intricate black mask as I situated it over my eyes. Mark thought I wore it to give myself a more mysterious appeal, but I needed that mask. It was the only way I could build the courage to go up on stage. It kept me hidden. It kept me safe.

On the outside, I looked like a sexy, confident woman, but on the inside, I was dying a little bit every time I went out on stage. But I could hide it. I had to.

The song built and when I heard my cue to enter the stage, I took a deep breath, filling my lungs, and blew out all my nerves. I wasn't Olivia Mae Conner anymore. I was Liv, and I ruled this stage.

My black high heels shined in the spotlight as I walked out onto the small black platform. The men catcalled as soon as they saw me, but I attempted to block them out. I focused on the beat of "Shameless" by The Weeknd, my song, and I let the lyrics sink into me.

My right hand met the pole at the center of the stage and the cold metal caused chill bumps to break out across my skin. Circling the pole slowly, I looked out into the room.

Most of the men wore sharp suits that were perfectly pressed and exquisitely fit. Long cigars hung from their mouths and glasses full of their choice of poison sat in their hands.

I made my way back around the front of the pole, and I quickly dropped down, my back against the cold metal, my thighs spread open, my body on display. I heard a few sharp inhales of breath, and I knew that I was doing my job. Hunger stared back at me in the eyes of the men that surrounded me.

I rolled my hips as I began to stand, but my footing faltered when I looked into the pair of green eyes that were staring at me from the center of the room. Undeniable lust looked back at me.

I blinked, my long eyelashes hitting my mask, and continued to dance. Standing, I bent at the hips and ran my hand down my leg. My hips rolled to the beat of the music, and my heart pounded at a much faster pace. He looked familiar to me, too familiar, but I couldn't get a good enough look from where I danced. But as I glanced back out into the crowd, I couldn't move my eyes away from him.

He looked dangerous. He reminded me of a bad habit. He was something I knew I shouldn't want, but I felt myself gravitating toward him regardless.

There was barely an inch of his skin that wasn't covered in tattoos. I couldn't make out what they were in the dark lighting, but I could see his tattooed hand wrapped around a crystal glass with each knuckle marked with ebony ink.

His gaze bore into me. He watched every swivel of my hips. He tracked my every move like a hunter ready to strike its prey.

My body knew the music and moved without me putting in much thought. My hips rolled, my hands caressed, and the men in front of me ate it up as if I was their last meal.

But I needed to get closer to him.

The need to know where I knew him from was overpowering. I stepped off the stage but didn't immediately make my way over to him. Instead, I took my time, giving each man in the room a closer look as I made my way to him. But I watched him. I searched the shadows that clouded his face for some resemblance of who he was.

It wasn't until I reached the man next to him that I truly got a good look. As soon as I took in his piercing green eyes, I knew why they looked so familiar to me. It was the same pair of eyes that had haunted my dreams for the last four years.

Parker fucking James.

From the way he was studying me, he thought he knew me as well, but he still hadn't figured it out. The last time I saw him, I was nothing more than a girl. My body was different. My hair was different. Hell, I was a completely different person.

I was no longer the girl with mousy brown hair and long gangly legs. I had finally figured out my body, and I was no longer ashamed of it. I didn't have a hesitant touch that begged him to teach me what to do anymore. My moves were calculated and assertive.

My hips rolled to the music and my knees brushed against his. I felt that small touch as if it had burned me. The flames licking up my legs and setting my entire body on fire.

My fingers fell to his trouser covered thighs, and I gently pushed them apart. My body rolled against his out of habit, and the strong spicy scent of him surrounded me. It was reminiscent of the Parker I used to know, but he smelled so much better now. He smelled like a man.

His hands lowered to the arms of the chair, and I watched his inked fingers as they clenched into fists. I flipped my hair against his chest and turned my back to him. I was practically sitting in his lap, and I took a shuddering breath while I had a momentary reprieve from him seeing my face.

I could feel how turned on he was against my ass, and that little piece of information fueled me. Parker was always the one in control. He was the powerful one, but not tonight.

My back pressed against his chest and my ass ground further against him as I rolled my body to the music. Fuck. He felt amazing.

His chest heaved below me and his harsh breath rushed out against my neck. It reminded me of four years earlier when I had given myself to him willingly, when I had practically begged him to make love to me. I closed my eyes against the memory. *Don't think about it, Liv. Don't let yourself go there.*

Leaning forward, I arched my back as I continued to grind against him. His hand ran up my spine, and a shiver chased his touch inch by inch.

"No touching," I whispered as I would to any other customer.

His hand clenched against my skin before it fell away.

"Take it off," his deep, gruff voice called out, barely heard over the music.

My trembling hands reached behind me and gripped the clasp of my bra. I could do this. Showing weakness in front of him wasn't an option.

My fingers pressed the fabric into my skin, but before I could release the hold of the clasp, Parker's hand covered mine.

His mouth leaned against my ear, and I almost died when I felt his warm breath rush out against my earlobe. "I meant the mask. Who are you?"

Chills ran through my body at his question. I was no one. Not to him. Not anymore. So instead of answering him, I rolled my hips a final time and moved to the man beside him.

He was still staring at me, and God, I wished I could move my eyes off him. I was on autopilot, moving through my routine without thought. But the feeling of a hand against the ribbon of my mask caused me to panic and search the face of the man in front of me as the mask fell to the floor.

Shame took over every other thought as I heard my name leave his lips.

"Livy?"

There were sharp inhales of breath around us, but I didn't dare move my gaze away from my brother's.

"Mason."

A glass crashed to the ground beside me, but I still didn't move. I couldn't face looking at Parker anymore. Not without my mask. He was too potent, and I needed to protect myself.

"What the fuck are you thinking?" Mason roared as he gripped my arm. He pulled me to a standing position, and it wasn't until that moment that I realized how naked I was in front of my brother. I covered my chest with my arms, but that only seemed to fuel his anger.

"So this is why you're too busy to come home? This is how busy you've been with your new job? You fucking lied to me." His eyes were black as the night sky as anger filled him.

His fingers dug into my skin as I watched the bouncer make his way over to us.

"Mason, you're hurting me," I whispered.

His fingers instantly loosened their grip, but he still held me close to him.

The bouncer, Hank, reached out for me, but Parker stepped in front of him.

"You need to move," Hank threatened. "I'm taking her out of here." He nodded his head in my direction.

"Over my dead body." The sound of Parker's voice stirred something inside me, and I had to remind myself that he was the same boy that broke my heart.

"It's okay, Hank."

Parker's back straightened and my brother pulled me closer to him, his body shielding mine.

"He's my brother." I pointed to Mason, and I could see the shock in Hank's eyes.

"I need to get Mark." He started heading toward the door, but I stopped him.

"You think you can just give me a few minutes. I promise I will handle it."

He looked hesitant as his eyes bounced back and forth between me and my brother, but eventually gave in. "Five minutes then I'm coming back."

I nodded my head then he made his way back out of the room.

"Why are you here?" I pulled my arm from my brother's grip and looked around the room at the combination of accusation and lust staring back at me.

"Why are we here?" Parker scoffed and ran his tattooed hands through his hair that had been perfectly styled before.

"Are you kidding me, Livy? Why are *you* here?" My brother's voice shook with fury.

Parker's name was on the tip of my tongue, but I knew that wasn't fair. I couldn't blame my decisions on him.

"It's my job, Mason. Why didn't you tell me you were coming to Atlanta?"

"When?" He threw his hands up in frustration. "You mean all those times I call you and you don't answer. I called you today."

I didn't have a response because he was right. I hated lying to him, so I avoided talking to him as much as I could.

"You all need to leave." I looked toward the door to make sure Hank wasn't coming back. I didn't want them to cause a scene. I couldn't afford to lose my job.

"We're not leaving here without you." It wasn't the words that surprised me but who they came from.

"You don't have a say, Parker." I stared up at him. He was still about six inches taller than me even in my heels and his green eyes were on fire.

"He's right," Mason growled. "You are coming home."

I searched the room full of his friends who were all staring at us but pretending not to. I didn't recognize any of them, and it hit me how far I had removed myself from my brother. I barely knew anything about him anymore.

Wanting to go home with him wasn't the problem. I just didn't want to get hurt again. Parker had practically destroyed me once and being around him made my chest ache. I couldn't risk losing myself to him again, but I couldn't tell my brother that. I had been nothing more than Parker's secret, and my brother would shit himself if he knew what happened. If he knew that Parker was the reason I ran.

So instead of telling him, I put a smile on my face and tried to avoid the topic altogether.

"Who's getting married anyways?" I looked around the room again. Some of the guys were covered in tattoos like Parker and some looked clean cut like my brother.

It wasn't until my gaze landed back on the two men that my world used to revolve around that I realized how fucked I really was. All it took was one word from Parker's lips.

"Me."

CHAPTER 2

THE INEVITABLE DROP

LIV

FOUR YEARS AND SIX MONTHS EARLIER

EVERYONE WAS LAUGHING at a joke Parker was telling. He was animated, using his hands as he spoke, and the group around him was eating it up.

I took a sip of my water since my brother was a party pooper and wouldn't let me drink like everyone else. Mason was only a year older than me, and we were all too young to drink. But he thought he was my dad and the only way he agreed to let me come to the party was if I swore I wouldn't drink.

Like I said, party pooper.

I watched Parker as he pushed his brown hair out of his eyes. His girlfriend, Madison, stood attached to his side, and she hadn't taken her eyes off him. I wanted to tell her to back off because Parker was mine.

Except he wasn't.

He was hers.

I was just a girl who was in love with him.

She giggled loudly at something he was saying, and I rolled my eyes. Parker was funny, but his joke wasn't *that* funny.

With every second that passed, I could feel the oxygen leaving the room. I was suffocating in my jealousy, and there was only so much I could take. Parker looked up at me when I stood, but his girlfriend quickly drew his attention back to her when she touched his arm. Her eyes flicked to me, and I could see the warning there. Parker was hers, and I better back off. It was loud and clear.

But she didn't need to worry about me. I didn't stand a chance.

The back deck creaked under my weight, and I filled my lungs with fresh air.

Keeping my feelings for Parker in check had become a full-time job, and it crushed me to watch him with another girl. It killed me.

There had been plenty of girls over the years too. He had been my brother's best friend for as long as I could remember, and there wasn't a time when I wasn't in love with him. It felt like it was the only thing I had ever known.

Everyone liked Parker. He was funny, athletic, and handsome as hell. But there were so many things about Parker that those other girls didn't see. He was a fiercely loyal friend, and he had my brother's back more times than I could count. He was also sweet. It wasn't a side of him that he let many people see, but I saw it. He treated his momma like she was a queen, and although he probably wouldn't admit it out loud, I knew he went once a week to visit his grandfather.

His art though. That was how I knew the true Parker.

I jumped when I heard the door open behind me, and I held my breath with hope that Parker came after me. But just like the bloom of hope that I always held in my chest, this one was destroyed just as quickly as it formed.

A head of shaggy blond hair poked out the door, and I

quickly recognized him as Thomas Alexander, a guy who graduated with my brother and Parker.

"Hey, Olivia." He walked out onto the porch before closing the door quietly behind him. I wanted to tell him that I hated when people used my full name, but for some reason, I stopped myself.

"Hey, Thomas. How are you?" I took a sip of my water to cover how awkward I felt being out here alone with him.

Thomas was cute. Really cute actually, but he wasn't Parker. I didn't get butterflies in my stomach when he walked into the room. I didn't hold my breath waiting for him to say my name.

"I'm good. I'm just in town visiting from school." He pushed his hair back out of his face, and I noticed how blue his eyes were for the first time.

Maybe this was what I needed. I couldn't get over my crush on Parker unless I tried to move on with someone else. Right?

"That's awesome. How is school going?"

"It's great. It's weird being so far away from home, but I love it. I'm in a fraternity and my brothers are cool as shit. We throw parties that are so much better than anything that's thrown in this town."

Blah. Blah. Blah.

I looked out over the deck railing and watched the moon's reflection beam against the ground. The moon was so grand and larger than life, and when I looked up in the sky and saw it surrounded by stars, it reminded me of Parker. He was so far out of my reach. I could admire him from afar just like everyone else except the stars. They were the only ones that were in the same realm as him. I would never be one of the stars. I would never be the girl who got Parker James.

"Did you hear me, Olivia?" Thomas's voice finally broke

through, and I realized that I hadn't been listening to a word he said.

"I'm sorry. What?" He had moved much closer to me when I wasn't paying attention, and he was only about a foot away now. I could easily reach out and touch him.

"Have you decided where you're going to go to school yet? You graduate in just a few months."

"Oh, school. Umm..." I tucked my hair behind my ear. I would be lying if I said that Parker wasn't the biggest factor in me deciding where I wanted to go. "I've been accepted to a few schools that I'm interested in, but I'll probably stay home and go the University of Tennessee."

"Really?" He snarled his lip and my back straightened.

"Yeah. I've been interested in the University of Tennessee for as long as I can remember. What's wrong with that?"

"There's nothing wrong with it. You are just so incredibly smart. I don't want to see you stuck in this town like a bunch of those losers in there." He hiked his thumb over his shoulder in the direction of the party that was still in full swing.

"Those guys aren't losers. Just because you go to an ivy league school doesn't mean you are any better than them." I crossed my arms and bit my lip between my teeth to stop myself from losing my temper.

"Actually, it does. It's practically the definition of being better than them." He smirked, and I wanted to smack him in his face that no longer looked the least bit attractive.

Before I got the chance, the back door burst open with a loud crash against the wall and Parker stepped out onto the porch.

"What the hell, Livy?" His voice was stern. "Mason and I have been looking for you everywhere."

"Obviously not everywhere. We've been out here for about fifteen minutes."

Parker snapped his gaze toward Thomas, and Thomas shrank back minutely. Maybe he was smarter than I gave him credit for.

"Come on, Livy." Parker held his hand out to me, and I instantly placed my hand in his. The warmth of his skin ran through me, and I could feel that small, innocent touch throughout my whole body.

Thomas stepped toward me, his body crowding mine, and blocked my path to get to Parker.

"What's your problem, Parker? We're just talking." There was a small part of me that was impressed Thomas had the balls to stand up to Parker. Not many guys did. His eyes were burning into Thomas and his muscles that clearly had about thirty pounds on Thomas were tense under his t-shirt.

"My problem is that you have no business being out here with Livy. She is too young for you and too good for you."

I peeked over Thomas's shoulder to look at Parker.

"That's rich coming from you, Parker. You think you're good enough for her? I'm in college. What are you doing? Doodling all your hopes and dreams?"

Parker's art wasn't doodles. It was phenomenal. He probably had more talent in his pinky finger than Thomas fully possessed. I opened my mouth to defend him, but he spoke before I could manage a sound.

"I'm not good enough for her either." His eyes glanced at me for a moment. "She deserves far more than anyone at this party can give her." My heart swelled and broke at the same time. "But I'm damn sure that you are going nowhere near her. So, I suggest you move out of the way or I'll put you on your ass."

"I'll think I'll leave it up to Olivia." Thomas looked over his shoulder at me, and he looked smug. "Do you want to stay with me or go with him?"

My answer was easy. It had been my answer for as long as I could remember, and I didn't feel like it would change anytime soon.

"Him."

Parker's pupils flared, but I wouldn't let myself believe it was anything more than what it was. He was planning for a fight, and a fight was coming.

Thomas moved away from me and the disgust on his face was clear. I barely even knew the guy so I wasn't really sure what his problem was.

"Are you serious, Olivia?"

I looked at him then back to Parker then back at him again.

"Yes?" I said it like a question. How did he think I would actually pick him over Parker?

"That's fine." He took a step closer to me and Parker mirrored his movement. "I always knew you were just a piece of trash like the rest of them."

"Fuck you." I took a step closer to him, but Parker was already there.

His arm reached out against me and pressed into my stomach. He pushed me behind him, somewhat forcefully, and I realized that his control was unraveling. Although I couldn't see Parker's face, I could clearly read the fear in Thomas's eyes. He tried to mask it with his venom, but it was too real to hide.

Before Thomas got a chance to say another word, Parker's fist landed across his jaw and knocked Thomas to the ground. Everything happened so quickly, but I felt like it happened in slow motion. I memorized the bunch of Parker's muscles as he struck and the trail of blood that ran from Thomas's lip as he fell.

Parker was on Thomas before his head even connected with the ground. He gripped his perfectly pressed collared shirt in his hands and pulled Thomas's face close to his. "Don't ever talk to Livy like that again." Thomas started to open his mouth, but Parker shook him by his shirt. "Better yet, don't ever talk to her at all. Don't look at her. Don't even breathe her name."

Parker shoved Thomas away from him, and I cringed at the loud echo from his head hitting the wood of the porch.

The green of Parker's eyes looked lethal as he stepped away from Thomas and made his way to me. There was a smattering of blood running down his knuckles, but I wasn't sure who it belonged to.

Parker grabbed my hand in his and pulled me behind him without saying a word. His anger was scary. He was uncontrollable, unpredictable, and so damn hot.

My breathing was hard, but it wasn't out of fear. I wanted Parker James. Every day it seemed to get worse and worse, and there was nothing I could do to stop it.

I followed him through the house as he pulled me along behind him. He was walking so fast that I was having a hard time keeping up with him. His tight grip on my hand was leaving a bite of pain, but I liked it. I would take his skin on mine any way I could get it.

He took us to a large sitting room that was completely unoccupied before he dropped my hand and started pacing the room. It was shocking how quickly I was affected by the loss of his touch.

He ran his hands through his hair, and I watched as the blood from his knuckles trailed down his fingers.

"Parker, you're hurt."

I reached out for his hand, and he let me take it. All four knuckles of his fist were busted open and the blood was definitely his.

"We need to clean this up."

"I'll be fine."

"But Parker..."

"I'll be fine." His tone was final. "Are you okay?"

"Me?" I pointed to my chest. "I'm not the one who just got into a fight."

"I know." He gripped both of my hands in his and butterflies took off in my stomach. We were standing so close to each other that I could feel the warmth of him. I could see the specks of gold that hid in the green of his eyes. His busted hand rose from mine and tucked a piece of my brown hair behind my ear. "But you are the one who Thomas just talked to like that."

"Like what?" The voice boomed through the room, and I gritted my teeth.

I loved my brother. I really did. I just had to keep repeating that over and over in my head. He was probably the best brother I could wish for, but he had the absolute worst timing. Whenever I thought something was about to happen between Parker and I, Mason would burst into the room and ruin any chance of what was about to happen. I didn't know if it was on purpose or not, but either way, his timing was impeccable.

"It's fine, Mason." I pulled my eyes away from Parker to look at my brother. Parker had widened the space between us as soon as my brother walked in, and he looked like he wanted to be anywhere but here.

"What happened?" Mason stepped closer to me, and as he stepped out of the doorway, I noticed a small blonde lingering by the door.

"Thomas Alexander ran his mouth, but I took care of it." Parker spit out the words as if he was disgusted to even say his name.

Mason looked at Parker, and I could see them speaking to each other without ever saying a word. It drove me crazy because I wanted to know what the hell they had to say. It was something they did often, and it pissed me off. When Mason seemed satisfied with his silent conversation with Parker, he patted his shoulder once.

"Are you okay?" Mason gripped my chin in his hand and his eyes ran over my face.

"I told you I'm fine."

"Then where were you? We were looking everywhere for you."

"Mason..." I sighed.

"Don't 'Mason' me. Where were you?"

I crossed my arms, and he matched my stance. He was stubborn, but I had been following in his footsteps my whole life. I could be stubborn too. I learned it from the best.

"Dude, back off of her." Mason's eyes snapped from mine to his best friend's. "Just give her some space. I think she's dealt with enough tonight."

Parker was standing up for me to my brother, and I couldn't hide the small smile on my face.

Mason took a deep breath and looked me over again. "Let's get out of here."

"But..." the small, forgotten blonde at the door piped up.

I had never seen her before, but I wasn't surprised. Mason didn't stay with one girl for long.

"We're going to have to have a rain check, doll." Mason smiled down at her, and I wanted to puke when I saw her melt before my eyes.

"I can take Livy home."

Parker's words shocked me, and they seemed to shock my brother as well.

"You sure, man?" Mason looked from the blonde back to me.

"Yeah. I've got nothing better to do."

Pain bloomed in my chest at his words, but I smiled the

same fake smile that I wore often when I was around him. Did he not see how bad his words affected me?

"Cool." Mason and Parker slapped hands and then Mason took off with the small blonde in tow.

"You ready?"

"Yeah." My voice was clipped, and Parker could tell. He gave me a strange look, and I internally flipped him off for saying he had nothing better to do.

"Okay..." he hesitated before he led the way out to his truck.

He opened the door for me, and I rolled my eyes at the part of me that was swooning at his chivalry. I was just as easy as the blonde with my brother.

The truck roared to life and he thumbed his phone for a few seconds before one of my favorite songs started playing through the speakers.

I watched the houses pass by us out the window so he couldn't see the smile on my face.

"Are you really not going to talk the whole way home?" He looked over at me quickly before returning his attention to the road.

"I'm just tired."

"Really, Livy? I know you're mad. I'm just not sure why." He chuckled softly, and even though it was my favorite sound in the world, it grated on my nerves in that moment.

"Don't worry about it. I'm sure you've got better things to do anyways." I knew I was being catty, but he hurt my feelings.

Asshole.

"Ahh. That's what this is about. You're really mad about that?" His hand ran over the steering wheel, and I watched the way his fingers softly bounced against the leather to the low beat of the music that was playing.

"I'm not mad. I'm hurt." I looked back out the window and

watched as we pulled into my driveway. The only light on in the house was the living room light that I had left on earlier, and when I looked up at my mom's dark bedroom window, I knew she still wasn't home.

"Fuck, Livy. I didn't mean to hurt your feelings." He put the truck in park and turned to face me.

"Like I said, don't worry about it, Parker." My hand gripped the door handle, but he put his hand over mine before I could open it.

"What did you want me to say?"

I looked at him but didn't answer because I didn't know. What did I expect from him? I knew where we stood. That didn't mean a girl couldn't be hopeful. That I didn't dream about the day he would say something like...

"Did you want me to tell him that I just needed a few more minutes alone with his baby sister?"

There was a sharp inhale of breath, and I realized it came from me.

His hand pressed against my cheek and softly swept the same piece of hair from earlier out of my face. "It just keeps falling, doesn't it?"

Yes.

I wanted to scream at him.

It falls and falls and falls, and so do I.

There was no use trying to stop either of us.

It was an inevitable drop, the kind that made your heart race and the butterflies in your stomach take off like a tornado, and no matter how hard I tried, it was impossible to stop the free fall.

He leaned closer to me, and breathing was no longer possible. I had thought about this moment for as long as I could remember. His breath blew out against my lips, and I traced my tongue there to try to capture the taste of him.

"Livy," he breathed out my name and my stomach clenched.

A shrill sound rang through the truck interrupting the moment, and when the two of us looked down at his phone that lay between us, all the butterflies in my stomach came to a sudden halt and the breath I was holding finally escaped.

Madison Smith lit up his screen and ruined everything.

CHAPTER 3

DIRTY LITTLE SECRET

PARKER

PRESENT

THERE WAS no way my bachelor party could get any more fucked up. When she came out onto the stage, I knew that she was by far the sexiest woman I had ever seen, but I also knew that I had seen her before. I just couldn't put my finger on it.

My dick hadn't been that hard since I was eighteen years old and she was begging me to take her virginity. I hadn't been this furious since the moment she ran away, or better yet, the moment I pushed her away. Every extreme in my life, every high and every low, had a story with her attached to it.

Seeing her like this, with her body on display for all these fucking men, I wanted to kill her or fuck her or God. What was I thinking? I was getting married.

Married.

To a woman I love.

Fuck. Fuck. Fuck.

Livy was still standing in front of her brother. She'd crossed her arms over her chest but that only seemed to enhance her breasts rather than hiding them. I searched the faces of my friends. All of them, with the exception of Mason, were looking at her like they wanted nothing more than to devour her, but I would take them all out. I didn't give a fuck if they were my friends or not. She was mine.

No. She had been mine once.

It was the same thing. They didn't get to touch her.

She was driving me insane in her tiny black lace bra and panties, and for a moment, I just appreciated her body. The Livy I knew, the Livy I loved, she was so different from this girl standing in front of me. She had always been beautiful. I had never seen a girl more beautiful than my Livy, but this girl was on a different playing field. She didn't look like the rebellious country girl who used to run around in boots and cutoffs. That Livy would have gawked at the three-inch heels she was wearing now.

Her hair was different. Her body was different. Everything was different, yet, she was the same. I could see it hiding behind the makeup and bravado.

And my chest fucking ached.

I turned from looking at her, trying to get my shit together, and noticed Brandon at my side. I had many friends in this world, but Mason and Brandon, they were my brothers. Nothing would ever come between us. Except if Brandon didn't quit looking at Livy like that. My hands shook with the urge to knock out one of my best friends.

I turned back to Livy, still fully on display, and pulled my jacket off and placed it around her shoulders. She stiffened when the fabric touched her skin, but I also knew she was thankful for the shield.

Her light brown eyes slid to mine as she pushed her arms in my jacket and pulled the engulfing fabric around her.

Her eyes. They were the same.

She had eyes that could see straight through me, no matter how hard I tried to hide from her, she saw. She always had.

"I swear to God, Livy. I'm not leaving here without you." She rolled her eyes, but Mason continued. "They will have to arrest my ass before I'll leave you."

Atta boy. I could see her resolve weakening.

"Can you at least let me tell my boss that I'm leaving and let me get my things?" She put her hands on her hips but my sleeves hung six inches past her fingertips.

"We'll be at the car." Mason pointed toward the illuminated red exit sign. "You have ten minutes, Livy."

She huffed, and I smiled.

She may have changed, but that spunky, rebellious attitude was the same Livy I had always known.

She marched her way back toward the stage and disappeared behind the curtain that had opened and wrecked my world only moments before.

My heart raced as I watched her vanish from my sight, but I reminded myself that she wasn't going to run again. She had nowhere to go when we are all here waiting for her. But most of all, I reminded myself that it wasn't my place to care.

I should be worried about Emily. I was marrying Emily, but as soon as Livy walked back into my world, everything became cloudy. It was harder to see Emily through the fog.

I tried to think about her lips, but Livy's cherry reds popped into my head. When I tried to think of her laugh, all the moments I shared with Livy came flooding back.

I pulled out my cell phone. I needed to look at a picture of Emily. I needed to get Livy out of my head. I had spent too many years thinking about that girl.

As soon as my screen lit up, I saw a text from Emily.

Don't fall in love with a stripper. ;) I love you! xoxo

And just like that, guilt flooded me. Emily was perfect. She was sweet and caring, and well, she was safe. I didn't worry that

Emily would get hurt and run. I didn't worry that I couldn't keep up with her. I just didn't have to worry with her.

She was beautiful, she loved me, and I needed to fucking remember that.

Instead, I slid my phone in my pocket and watched Livy as she made her way out of the strip club carrying a small gym bag. She looked upset, and I was immediately on alert.

But when I started stepping toward her, her brother did the same, and I remembered that it wasn't my place to comfort her.

She was dressed in a pair of ripped up jeans and a simple black tank top. She still looked hot as fuck, but she looked more like the girl I used to know.

"Well," she held out her arms, one of which was carrying my suit jacket, "I guess I'm all yours since you got me fired."

Mason scooped her up in his arms and held her tightly against him. I had never been more jealous of my best friend, but Livy wasn't looking at him. She was staring at me but looked away the moment I noticed, and the vulnerability I saw there completely fucked with my head.

She threw my jacket to me when he finally put her down then wiped her palms against her jeans. "So, what are we doing? This is a bachelor party, right?" Her eyes flicked to me, but then a fake ass smile formed on her face. "Let's go have some fun."

IT WAS MY BACHELOR PARTY, and I was pretty sure I was the person having the least amount of fun. Livy had all my boys eating out of the palm of her hand as she told jokes and entertained them with memories of her and her brother. She seemed careful not to bring up stories that included me, and fuck if that didn't hurt.

We had been at some club for the last hour. I didn't even know the name of the place. I was too busy watching her as she linked her arm with Brandon's and walked in the door. She had always known how to push my buttons, and it seemed that she hadn't forgotten.

So instead of enjoying my time with my boys, I was sitting in a booth with a glass of whiskey in my hand as I tracked her movements like a stalker.

"What's up, sour puss?" Brandon fell into the seat beside me, and I gave him the death stare when my liquor spilled out onto my pants.

"Really, man?" I wiped at my pants with a napkin, little white rolls of paper sticking to the fabric, and listened to him chuckle.

"What's gotten into you tonight? You look like you've either seen a ghost or like you really wish that ghost would come dance on your lap again."

I smacked him in his chest, and he laughed before rubbing the spot with his tattooed hand.

"What the hell was that for?"

"You know what it was for, asshole." I took a large drink of my whiskey and reveled in the burn.

"She's the one who got away, huh?" He nodded his head toward Livy where she was laughing at the bar after downing another shot.

"Something like that."

"What are you going to do?"

"What do you mean 'What am I going to do'?" I finally turned my gaze from Livy to look at my best friend.

"Well we both know that Mason isn't going to leave here without her. How are you going to handle it?" He was watching me. The usual jokester Brandon was gone, and he was being serious. He was worried about me.

"I'm going to go home to my fiancée and forget about Livy like I've been doing for the last four years."

He scoffed at my answer, and I narrowed my eyes at him.

"You can try to fool everyone else," he said before sipping his drink, "but I can see through you. You haven't forgotten about that girl for one second."

"I don't care if you believe me because it's the truth. The moment Emily walked into my life, I forgot all about Livy."

His face was forming into this stupid ass grin that he always did when he thought he was being really funny or that he had an epic plan. It was a look that made me fucking nervous.

"Well here's your chance to prove it," he spoke against the rim of his glass before looking away and trying to hide his smile.

"Hey, Parker." My name was slightly slurred, and when I looked over at Livy swinging her legs on the booth across from me, it was easy to tell that she was well on her way to hammered.

"Hey, Livy." I cleared my throat.

"Ugh." She rolled her eyes. "Don't call me that. I go by Liv now."

"Whatever you say, Livy."

She narrowed her eyes at me and I smiled. I missed this. The back and forth. The push and pull.

"So, am I going to get to meet your fiancée when I get back?" She had her brave face on, but I could see the vulnerability in her eyes. I had always been able to see it.

"If that's what you want."

"What's her name?"

I started to answer, but she held up her hand to cut me off.

"No. Wait. Let me guess." She tapped her index finger against her chin playfully, and I felt each beat against my chest.

"Veronica. No. No. Jasmine?" She watched me for a reaction, but I didn't give her one. My best friend though, that asshole was chuckling at her antics.

"It has to be something exotic. I mean only the best for Parker James, right?" She was making a fool of herself, but I was letting her. This was the most she had spoken to me in four years. Four fucking years.

"Please tell me it isn't Francesca." She put her hand dramatically against her chest.

"It's not Francesca," I said calmly.

"Well I give up. What's her name?" She leaned forward like she was really interested, but I doubted she truly was.

"Emily." I almost choked on her name. "Her name is Emily."

She closed her eyes briefly. She probably thought I wouldn't notice, but she had been drinking and she was showing more of herself than she normally would.

"I'm surprised." She opened her eyes and looked straight at me. "Emily is a good girl name. You never really had a thing for good girls."

"Didn't I?" My gaze didn't waver from hers, and I could tell she was getting nervous. She probably had some grand plan in her head before she made her way over here, and it wasn't going quite like she thought it would. "You were a good girl, weren't you?"

I took another sip of my whiskey, and I watched as her anxiety morphed into anger.

"You didn't have a thing for me, Parker. I was nothing more than your dirty little secret." She stood from her seat, and I watched her movements as she came closer to me. Her hand landed on the back of the booth behind my head and her face was only inches from mine. I could smell cranberry juice and vodka on her lips, and I wanted nothing more than to lean forward and taste it as well.

I felt intoxicated by her proximity, the whiskey having nothing on her, and it made me forget everything. I forgot that I hurt her, that she hurt me, that she ran, but more than anything, I forgot that I wasn't hers anymore.

She stared into my eyes as she spoke the next words, but my gaze bounced between her eyes and her full lips.

"I may have been a good girl then, but you destroyed every piece of her. I actually feel bad for Emily, because you, Parker James, are where good girls go to die."

Her words sank into me as she pushed off the booth and turned her back to me.

They settled into my chest, taking root exactly where she wanted them.

"You are so fucking screwed."

I looked over at Brandon. I had completely forgotten he was there, but he was right, I was completely fucked.

CHAPTER 4

SOME PIECE OF ASS

PARKER

FOUR YEARS AND GIVE AND A HALF MONTHS EARLIER

I COULDN'T STOP THINKING about her.

She had been avoiding me for two weeks, and it was driving me insane.

Every time Madison walked by, I compared how she looked to Livy.

Every time she spoke, I thought about how much more Livy and I had in common.

It was shitty. I knew that, but I couldn't stop.

And I tried, believe me, I tried everything.

I thought that maybe I could fuck her out of my mind.

When Madison wouldn't stop talking about some girl she hated, I just kissed the shit out of her to get her to shut up. But instead of thinking about her lips against mine, I imagined they were Livy's. Madison's lips tasted like strawberries and were sticky from some crap she put on them. I imagined that Livy's were soft and smooth.

When I grabbed Madison's hips, I thought of the curvier ones that belonged to Livy.

It worked for a while. Replacing Madison in my mind with the one I really wanted. I knew what kind of dirt bag that made me, but I couldn't help it.

Madison was into it too. At least, she was into me. Because it was the most I had ever been into her.

She clung to me like she never wanted to let me go, and when I thought about Livy doing the same, I had never been so turned on in my life.

But that all went downhill.

Because Madison ruined it. Fuck. I ruined it.

With just three little words. Words that typically meant nothing when you're nineteen-years-old, but as soon as the words left her lips, I knew I couldn't go any further. I may not have loved Madison, but she didn't deserve what I was doing to her. She didn't deserve to be replaced with someone else in my mind.

So instead of repeating her breathless words back to her, I gripped her arms softly and pushed her off me. I could see the rejection in her eyes staring back at me, and it hurt, but not as much as when I saw it from Livy.

When Livy jumped out of my truck after our almost kiss, it gutted me.

I didn't even feel a fraction of that for Madison, and that's how I knew that I couldn't continue this any longer.

"What's wrong?" Her words were broken, and I hated that I was hurting her.

"I can't do this anymore, Madison."

"Is it because I said I love you? I can take it back. I didn't even mean it." She was scrambling to save what we had, and I could see the desperation in her eyes.

"It's not that. I just can't do this anymore." I rubbed my hand over the back of my neck and tried to avoid looking at her, like a coward.

"This is about her. Isn't it?" Her voice was no longer soft and broken but full of fire and venom.

"Who?" As soon as the word left my mouth, I knew it was a mistake. Both of us knew exactly who she was talking about.

"What are you going to do, Parker?" She paced in front of me, venom spilling from her lips, the real Madison making an appearance. "Ruin your lifelong friendship over some piece of ass."

"She's not some piece of ass, Madison," I sighed. "I'm sorry. Okay? I didn't mean for this to happen."

"No. It's not okay." She pointed her perfectly manicured finger at me. "You will fucking regret this, Parker. I promise you." And with that she stormed out of my room and out of my house.

...

When I emerged from my bedroom, my mother was sitting on the couch with a book in her hand. She had a sly smile on her face, and I could only imagine what was coming next.

She set her book down softly in her lap and pushed her dark brown hair out of her face. When her green eyes that perfectly matched mine looked up at me, I could see that she was trying her hardest not to give herself away.

"Let's hear it, Mom." I plopped down in the chair across from her.

"What do you mean?" She placed her hand on her chest in mock innocence. "I was just going to ask you why Madison ran out of here crying. What did you do to that poor girl?"

"I broke up with her."

And just like that, my mom's face lit up.

"Oh, thank God." She slumped her shoulders. "I didn't know if I could fake being nice to her for one more day."

"Mom!" I laughed.

"What? It's the truth. All that fake laughing and fake tan. A mother can only take so much."

"Mom, you get spray tans too." I pointed out stupidly.

"Yes, but I have a wonderful soft glow about me." She ran her hand down her arms like she was modeling gloves. "That girl is orange."

She stood from the couch to walk to the kitchen and I followed her. The smell of vanilla invaded me as she passed by me, and it was one of my favorite smells in the world. It smelled like home.

"Why didn't you tell me how much you hated her?" I sat down at the bar as she started pulling pans out from the cabinets.

"Hate is a strong word. I would go with..." She tapped her finger against the counter. "Major dislike. Plus, you're still young. I know that you're still playing the field as you kids like to say." She wagged her eyebrows at me and I died a little inside.

"Mom." I chuckled.

"If you married her, I would have just disowned you. At least until you had kids because they would definitely need their Nana. Can you imagine what your kids would have looked like?" My mom shuddered. "They probably would have popped out with orange skin, platinum blonde hair, and a French manicure."

"You could never disown me. I'm your baby boy." I leaned back in my chair and grinned at her.

"That's true, but I would try to beat some sense into you." She waved her spatula in the air in my direction. "Or get Livy to help me."

"How could Livy help you?" I leaned forward resting my chin in my hand.

"That girl has you wrapped around her little finger. You just haven't figured it out yet."

But I was all too aware of the effect Livy had on me. I just didn't know what I was going to do about it.

CHAPTER 5

DOUBLE TROUBLE

LIV

PRESENT

I NEVER REALLY UNDERSTOOD WHY people called it a hangover because I didn't feel hungover. I felt like I was dying.

By the time Mason and I had managed to pack up my sparse apartment and drive back to Tennessee, I didn't care where I ended up. I just needed painkillers, a pitch-black room, and some peace and quiet.

So, that's what I did for the first couple days. I settled into the guest room of my brother's beautiful house, and I hid out.

It felt weird to be in his space. The whole house fit him so perfectly. My brother worked in construction, and you could see the craftsmanship in every aspect of his home. But it was also so easy to see that no one other than a bachelor lived there.

He had a large bath that I soaked in for hours trying to rid myself of my embarrassment from the night of Parker's bachelor party.

I had been half naked.

In front of Parker, in front of my brother, and in front of all their friends.

I buried my head under the water and screamed out my frustration. I could remember bits and pieces of the night and the things I had said to Parker, but the more I remembered, the more I wanted to forget.

He seemed so angry with me. The whole night he watched my movements with a sour look on his face, but I didn't care what he thought of me.

At least, I wished I didn't.

He was furious when I pulled Brandon onto the dance floor and ground against him, and he looked like he was ready to kill me when I licked salt off his friend Josh's hand before throwing back a shot of tequila.

After that everything became blurrier. I remembered arms lifting me in the air and carrying me home after I could no longer walk on my own, but I couldn't remember whose they were.

When I woke up to Mason packing my apartment, I prayed that I was imagining things and that the night never really happened, but unfortunately, it had. I tried to think of every reason in the world why I shouldn't come home with Mason, but everything I came up with revolved around Parker.

So instead of begging my brother to leave me behind, I came up with a game plan. Really, it was more like a ground rule.

Avoid Parker James at all costs.

Simple.

Or at least I thought.

I managed to follow my ground rule for one day.

On the second day of my hiatus, my mother showed up at the door while my brother was at work. I loved my mom. I really did, but I really loved being about three hours away from her.

"Hey, Mom." I squinted out the front door into the sunlight.

"Oh God, Olivia." She pulled me into her arms, and I stiffened. "I'm so happy you're home."

"Yeah. Me too." I pulled the long sleeves of my shirt over my hands.

She pranced into my brother's home, setting her oversized purse down on the bar, and made herself at home.

Her hair was the same dark brown shade as mine, but that was where the similarities ended. She was dressed in some extravagant hot pink dress and a pair of black heels, and she didn't look like she was the mom of two adults.

"What have you been up to?" She pulled two bottles of water out of the refrigerator. When it took me longer than a second to answer, she spoke over me. It was something that I could always count on her for. "I can't wait for you to meet my boyfriend, Peter. You are going to love him."

Taking a sip of my water, I nodded my head. I'd met plenty of my mom's boyfriends throughout the years, and sure, I liked some of them. They were all typically nice to Mason and me, but they were also not around for very long.

That was the thing about my mom. She needed a man in her life, but she never seemed to find one that could hold her attention for long. Or maybe it was the other way around. I didn't really know. All I knew was that the constant influx of men tended to leave me and Mason to our own devices, and we preferred it that way.

We stuck together, we took care of each other, and we were each other's best friends. Until I left.

"Are you dating anyone, Livy?"

"No, Mom."

She fingered a piece of my hair that I hadn't brushed since I had gotten out of the bath the day before. "You're not going to be young forever, you know."

"I'm well aware." I rolled my eyes.

My mom talked some more about herself, her boyfriend, and her new purse for a good hour before I managed to get her out of the house. And when the door shut behind her, I felt hungover again.

By the time Mason made it home from work, I was chin deep in a fluffy white blanket on his couch binge watching *Game of Thrones*.

Because Jon Snow.

"Is this all that you've been up to today?" He pushed my feet out of his way and sat down next to me.

"No. I managed to paint my nails." I wiggled my freshly painted black toenails at him. "Then Mom showed up."

He winced and I knew he felt my pain without me having to say anything else. "Sorry. I tried to push her off as long as I could. I didn't know she would drop by today."

"It's not your fault. I had to face her sooner or later." I shrugged.

"What did you, um?" He scratched his head, looking nervous and totally out of character for my brother. "What did you tell her you've been doing?"

"This is Mom we're talking about, Mason. We only talked about her."

He nodded his head in understanding before grabbing my bottle of water off the table and taking a drink.

"Well, get ready." He stood from the couch, stretching his muscles. "We're going out to dinner tonight. You've been cooped up in this house too long."

I groaned, but he was right. I couldn't stay locked up in this house forever. Even if I wanted to.

...

This was not what I expected. If I had known we were meeting people for dinner, I would have dressed better, or you know, not have come.

But it was too late for that now. When we walked into the restaurant, Mason passed the hostess and headed straight for the back. As soon as I saw the table filled with three other people, panic filled me.

Brandon smiled at me when he saw us approaching, and I made quick work to grab the seat next to him. Because on the other side of him was a pretty girl with light blonde hair and bright blue eyes. She wasn't what bothered me though; it was Parker's arm against the back of her chair.

He was staring at me as Mason pulled out my seat, and I tried to avoid looking at him in his plain black t-shirt that looked far too insanely hot against the backdrop of his tattoos.

The table was silent when we first sat down, and I avoided looking at anyone except for my brother.

But Brandon didn't let that fly. He pulled my chair closer to his and pulled me into his side. "There's my drinking buddy. How are you feeling?"

"Finally getting over my hangover after trying to keep up with you." I nudged him with my elbow.

"I told you, girl. You should have listened instead of being so competitive."

I laughed because he was right. I never backed down from a challenge.

"Livy," Parker's voice pulled me from my conversation with Brandon, and he sounded nervous. "This is my fiancée, Emily."

Emily smiled sweetly at me and gave me a little wave. A perfect little wave with her perfectly pink nails. I was such a bitch for judging her. She looked nice as could be, but she didn't look right next to Parker.

"Hi, Emily. It's nice to meet you."

"You too." She seemed far too excited to meet me. "I've heard so much about you."

My gaze slid to Parker, but he was swallowing down half his beer. I doubted she had truly heard that much about me. At least not the parts that mattered.

"I've heard a lot about you as well. Are you excited about the wedding?" *Why the fuck did I just ask that?*

"Yes!" Her voice went up a few octaves, and I think everyone at the table winced. "Parker has been amazing." She looked up at him, and I looked at Brandon's glass in front of him. I wondered if he would notice if I quickly chugged his whiskey. "But you've known him forever." Her voice broke through my thoughts. "You know how great he is."

"Oh yeah. For sure."

Brandon snorted softly beside me, but Emily just nodded her head.

The rest of dinner seemed to go the same way. Emily talked about the wedding while everyone else listened. We all interjected ohs and ahs where necessary, but I was itching to get out of there. I wasn't too keen to hear all the details of Parker's wedding. A wedding that one-day ago, I had envisioned myself in.

It seemed like a joke now. How naïve I was. How idiotic.

"So Liv, have you thought about what you're going to do for a job?"

Brandon's question caught me off guard because I hadn't really thought about it at all.

"Umm, I'm not sure yet. I guess I need to start looking." I laughed.

Mason pulled me into his side. "No rush."

"Well I'm looking for a receptionist, if you're interested."

"Really?" I perked up because working with Brandon sounded awesome. The two of us had so much fun together.

"Yeah." The server walked up to our table and interrupted us. Brandon leaned in closer to me to talk over her. "I'll call you tomorrow to talk details."

Parker was staring at him, but Brandon just took a swig of his drink and smirked at him.

Then Parker lifted his own drink and I saw a small tattoo located on the inside of his left wrist. A tattoo that was all too familiar. A small, insignificant tattoo that most people looked over, but not me. I knew that tattoo because I drew it. I doodled it in one of his books over four damn years ago, and now it was on his body. And I couldn't take my eyes off it.

"Livy, are you seeing anyone right now?" Emily's voice caught me off guard, and I pulled my eyes away from Parker to look at her.

"I'm sorry. What?"

"Are you dating anyone?"

Why did everyone keep asking me that?

"No. Not right now." I avoided looking at Parker.

"I have a friend that I think you would hit it off with. He's cute, and he's a flight attendant."

Brandon snorted at my side. "I think you're trying to set him up with the wrong friend."

"What do you mean?" Emily looked at Brandon, clearly annoyed.

"He's a male flight attendant. I think you'd have a better chance at setting him up with Mason."

I choked on my water when I couldn't help but laugh.

"Fuck you, man," my brother called out at the same time Emily said, "You're such an asshole, Brandon."

Brandon shrugged his shoulders before winking at me. "I'm

just trying to save Livy some heartbreak. Can you imagine finding out the man you were in love with was actually in love with another man?"

"It would be devastating." I chuckled and Emily rolled her eyes. "Especially if he fell in love with my brother."

"I'm not gay." Mason slammed his hand on the table, and Brandon and I leaned into each other laughing.

"You two are going to be trouble together," Mason grumbled as he threw back the rest of his drink.

Brandon put his arm around my shoulder and Parker watched him like a hawk.

"Maybe you and Brandon should date," Emily said sarcastically, but Brandon and I looked up at each other.

I wasn't attracted to Brandon. Was he hot? Hell yes, but from the moment I met him, I knew we were going to be great friends. We were too much alike. Would we make a good couple? No. Would we make the greatest dynamic duo ever? Absolutely.

"I don't think Livy could handle me." Brandon was grinning at me, and it was impossible not to feed off his energy.

"Oh, Brando." I patted his cheek. "Go ahead and believe that, sweetheart."

"I can do this thing with my tongue," Brandon started, but Parker interrupted him.

"You do realize her brother is sitting right there, right?"

"Mason is your brother?" Brandon put his hand against his chest in fake shock.

"He is." I laughed.

"Well this is just tragic." He put my hand in his. "Best friends then?"

"Do we get a secret handshake?" I raised an eyebrow.

"What kind of barbarian do you take me for? Of course, we'll have a secret handshake. Don't worry, Parker." He looked up at his friend who was still watching us. "I'll keep it clean since her brother is right there."

Parker rolled his eyes, and I decided that Brandon and I were going to be great friends. If I couldn't avoid Parker while I was here, I could at least piss him off with his best friend.

CHAPTER 6

HE WAS THE ONLY THING I SAW

LIV

FOUR YEARS AND GIVE AND A HALF MONTHS EARLIER

PARKER WAS ACTING WEIRD. I had been avoiding him since the almost kiss, but today, he seemed to have a different plan. Because he wouldn't get out of my space. No matter where I moved, he seemed to mirror me.

We had been at the lake all day with my brother and some of their friends, and it was a good day. Parker had laid his towel out next to mine and his eyes were glued to me as I pulled off my tank top and blue jean shorts.

But I didn't care. At least that was what I was telling myself.

He watched every movement of my hands as I spread sunscreen over my skin, but I attempted to avoid looking at him. I put on my large sunglasses as he pulled out his sketch-book, but I avoided looking down as the pencil in his hand moved rapidly against the paper.

His gaze kept flicking to me, and when I couldn't take it anymore, I lay on my stomach and tried to relax in the warm summer sun.

The sun heated my skin, and as badly as I hated to admit it, the feel of Parker beside me made everything else disappear.

"Hey, man. Where's Madison?" some guy asked, causing me to stir.

My face was smooshed against my towel, and I was pretty sure there was a small amount of drool trailing down my chin. But my ears perked up at the mention of her.

"I couldn't tell you," Parker said without much thought.

"What, you can't keep your woman in line?" I rolled my eyes at the idiotic comment.

"She's not my woman anymore." Parker paused and my heart leaped out of my chest. "We broke up yesterday."

He broke up with her.

He broke up with her.

Did she break up with him?

Did he break up with her for me?

The mound of questions started rolling through my mind. Was it because of our almost kiss? Did it have absolutely nothing to do with me?

Instead of showing how interested in the answers I really was, I kept my head down against my towel and pretended to do nothing but bathe in the sun. But my heart was beating out of my chest.

After a few minutes, Parker finally broke the silence.

"You don't have anything to say?"

I wasn't sure if he was talking to me, but I peeked my eyes open and looked up at him through my arms.

"Yes. I'm talking to you." He leaned closer to me and I breathed in the scent of his cologne mixed with the sunshine.

"Why would I have anything to say?" I sat up, stretching my arms above my head causing his eyes to drop to my chest.

"You're good at a lot of things, Livy, but lying isn't one of them." He smirked, the right side of his mouth slightly higher than the left.

"Well what do you want me to say?" I pulled my hair out of my ponytail and shook it out.

"Tell me what you think." He was watching me closely, and I loved it. I fucking loved every second of it.

He still had his sketchbook in his hand. He always did. He was constantly drawing and doodling. Instead of answering him, I reached out and pulled it away from his chest. The drawing was a portrait. Something that he must have been working on for quite some time due to the intricate lines and shading. As I stared at my reflection on the paper, I didn't recognize the girl in front of me.

Half of my face looked normal, what the rest of the world saw, what I saw, but the other half was covered in flowers, wings, and bursts of wild lines. There was no order. It was chaotic and beautiful and ran off the page. You couldn't tell where she began and where she ended.

"It's beautiful." I ran my finger lightly down the page, tracing the line of my nose.

"You're beautiful." He was staring at me in a way he never had before.

He tucked a piece of hair behind my ear before his eyes skirted to my brother.

Did he want me to be happy that he and Madison broke up? Would it really change anything? We still had my brother to worry about.

But not right now, Mason was being Mason, and he was on the side of the ledge about to jump in the lake. I'm sure all the girls waiting below would be more than impressed by him, and he knew it too.

"Do you want to go for a swim?" I said breathlessly.

Parker stood and reached his hand out for me. I placed my

hand in his much larger one, and he followed me to the edge of the water.

The cool water hit my overheated skin as I dipped my toes into the lake. Parker was right behind me. I could feel him. Whether it was the heat of his body or his presence alone, I knew he was there, and when I leaped into the water headfirst, I knew he would follow me.

And when I came up for air, he was the first thing I saw.

He was the only thing I saw.

His hand slid against my hip under the water, and even though it was ninety degrees outside, chills bumps covered my skin. I could feel the calluses on his fingers from him constantly having a pencil in his hand.

He wrapped his other hand around mine, intertwining our fingers. Our exchange hidden under the dark water of the lake.

"What are we doing, Parker?" I whispered even though no one else was around us.

"I don't know." His hand tightened against mine. "But I can't stay away from you any longer."

CHAPTER 7

FRIEND ZONED

PARKER

PRESENT

BRANDON WAS A FUCKING IDIOT. Was he one of my best friends? Yes. Did he enjoy making my life miserable for his own sick enjoyment? Fuck yes.

He called me yesterday to tell me that he offered Livy a job and she took it. When I asked him if he told her that I owned half the business, he just laughed.

Of course, he didn't.

He knew it would be torture for me to work with her. He also thought it would be a good source of entertainment for him. What he didn't know though? Livy and I weren't a game.

But the thing about Brandon was he thought he knew better than anyone else.

Emily? He hated her with me. He said that she stifled me. Whatever the fuck that was supposed to mean.

When I told him I was proposing to her, he literally cringed. When I told him that she said yes, he voiced how crazy he thought I was.

But I wasn't crazy. Was Emily safe? Yes. No doubt. But I

didn't see anything wrong with playing it safe. Emily and I were different, sure. She had perfectly unmarked cream skin that was always incredibly soft and smooth. Me? My skin was covered in so much ink that I could barely remember what my skin looked like without it.

She rarely cursed and always made a face when expletives flew out of my mouth, but I tried to tame it down in front of her. Which annoyed the fuck out of Brandon.

But I knew what to expect out of Emily. I knew what a day with her looked like, even if it did look the same almost every day. She wasn't spontaneous, she didn't make rash decisions, and I wasn't scared that she would break my heart.

Was that a completely fucked up reason to marry someone? Sure. But she was my safety net.

And I loved her. I really did.

When I met Emily, I wasn't in a good place. I was drinking all the time, partying more than I was working, and thinking about Livy every second of the day.

But then I saw Emily. She didn't block Livy out of my mind completely, but she seemed a little fuzzier as each day passed. Then there were moments when I was with her, that I didn't see Livy at all, and I felt like I could actually breathe.

But I couldn't explain that shit to Brandon. He would call me a pussy and tell me that breathing wasn't a good enough reason to marry someone.

But he had never suffocated before. And until you feel it, the loss of air, the panic crawling through your skin, the desperation to inhale just one more time, you could never understand what it was like.

Emily was breathing, and I would never take the easy push and pull for granted again.

Like when I walked in the door of Forbidden Ink, my shop,

the place I had built with Brandon brick by brick, I could feel the lack of oxygen before I even saw her.

Forbidden Ink was my sanctuary. Tattooing, sketching, drawing, that was where I was one hundred percent at home. I could have a million things running through my head, but as soon as I put on some music and held a pencil or gun in my hand everything else melted away.

I was good at it. I wasn't being cocky, it was my one thing in this world, and I fucking rocked it. Brandon was just as good. That's why I went into business with him. We were two no-name apprentices who worked our asses off every single day. We bonded over our hard work and our artwork, and when it finally came time for us to do our own thing, we didn't even consider doing it with anyone else.

Livy was sitting behind the front desk when I walked in the door. Her head was down and her brow was furrowed, it was the face she had always made when she was hard at work. When the door chimed, she looked up quickly, a smile replacing the frown, but as soon as she saw it was me instead of a customer, the smile fell again.

"Hey, Parker." She looked back down at her paperwork in front of her. "What are you doing here?"

I would be lying if I said that it didn't feel a little bit good to know that I had something over her. Or at least that I knew something she didn't. Because she would be pissed when she found out.

Instead of answering her question, I asked one of my own. "Hey, Livy. How's the first day going?"

"It's good so far." She nodded her head. "Brandon really hasn't given me much to do yet though. He said he's waiting until his partner gets here." She pointed down at the pages in front of her. "I was just looking through some of their work. It's phenomenal. Did you get yours done here?" She motioned toward the ink that marred my skin.

"Most of it, yeah."

She nodded her head, but looked back down at the image in front of her. It was a drawing of mine. It was an anatomical heart, drawn in black and white. Intricate lines and shading. But half the heart was an explosion of colors, butterflies and flowers busting from the lines creating chaos and life.

Wild at heart. The title written below it.

It was one of my favorite drawings to date, but regardless of how many people asked for it, I always said no. I couldn't seem to part with it.

"This one is amazing." She took a deep breath and I held mine.

She turned the page over, looking for a signature I presumed, and I prayed she couldn't read mine. "I want this." She looked up at me. "Is that crazy? I just saw this and I want it tattooed on my body. Maybe working here wasn't such a good idea." She laughed softly, one of my favorite sounds in the world. "Do you think Brandon will tattoo this on me?"

I couldn't lie to her, not about my art. "That's not Brandon's." I pointed down at the page that I had spent countless hours drawing. "It's..."

But before I could get the rest of the words out of my mouth, the door to the back of the shop busted open and Brandon walked through with a shit eating grin on his face.

"Oh good." He rubbed his hands together. "I see you've finally met my partner."

I watched her for her reaction, but it wasn't quite what I was expecting. She closed her eyes, breathed through her nose, and her black fingernails gripped my drawing, creasing it a bit on the sides.

I expected her to scream at me, or hell, I don't know, throw something. But she didn't.

She opened her eyes and stared down at my drawing for a few more moments before she put it back in its place and closed the portfolio. Only then did she look up at me, and there was a flash of betrayal that always seemed to rest there when she looked at me.

"Brandon, can I talk to Parker alone for a minute?" She didn't look at him when she spoke. She just stared directly at me.

"Sure." I could hear the laughter in his voice, but I didn't dare look away from her.

When we heard the door shut again, she finally released a deep, shuddering breath, and it was as if I could feel it filling my own lungs. It was the deepest breath I had taken since she stole it so many years ago.

"I need this job, Parker."

I nodded my head, but she wasn't finished.

"I had no intentions of ever coming home, and I sure as hell didn't plan on being anywhere near you." That one stung, but I understood. I hadn't planned on being around her either. "If you can be civil, so can I. I'll do my job then I'll go home. I won't be in your hair or your business."

"Livy, you don't have to convince me. If you want the job, it's yours. We're completely different people than we used to be." That was an almost truth. "We can be friends."

I watched her wince. That same fucking line having left my mouth before, but this time I actually meant it. I was man enough to be able to work around her every day. Would it be difficult? Sure, but it wasn't something I couldn't handle.

I would just need to repeat that mantra in my head every day. I can handle this. I can handle this. I can handle this.

Because despite everything, the idea of being around her, of getting to know who she was now, it excited me more than I was willing to admit.

"Okay." She nodded her head as if she was convincing herself. "Friends."

"Friends," I repeated the word. It tasted foreign on my tongue, but mixed with the intoxicating scent of her I could swallow anything.

CHAPTER 8

ROCK STAR

PARKER

FOUR YEARS AND FIVE AND A HALF MONTHS EARLIER

I never really did plan things out. I just knew that I had to see her and there wasn't any other option.

I guess there never really was.

Her brother had plans with some new girl he met the night before. I knew because he told me in sordid details how amazing her rack was and what he planned on doing to her tonight.

That was the thing about Mason. He was an amazing guy. The best guy I knew. My best friend. But he was also a bit of a manwhore. Tonight, I was thanking God for that.

Her mother wasn't home when I pulled into the driveway, and I wasn't surprised. I knocked on the door, which felt incredibly awkward since it may have been the first time I had knocked on their door in over ten years.

I could see her through the glass of the front door. Her hair was on top of her head in a messy bun, she was wearing a pair of flannel pajama pants and a tank top, and a spoon was hanging out of her mouth, which probably had icing on it. She opened the door with her brow scrunched.

She pulled the spoon from her mouth, and just as I expected, I saw remnants of vanilla icing. "Did you just knock?" She looked at the door like maybe it was broken.

"Yes. I did. Would you like to go out with me, tonight?"

Her eyes widened at my question, and she looked so fucking adorable. I couldn't stand not to touch her. I reached my hand out and wiped the icing off her bottom lip before tasting it on my own tongue.

She held her breath when my skin touched hers, but I watched her chest shudder when I put my finger in my mouth. It tasted like vanilla icing and something even sweeter, and I was dying to put my lips on her to chase it.

"I need to change." She looked down at her clothes before she reached on the top of her head and felt her bun.

"Well hurry up. We have plans."

She smiled at me. That fucking smile that made me feel weak in the knees before she took off running up the stairs to her room.

I had been in her house so many times, hell, I practically lived here some days, but I had never been here like this. I had never been here with her instead of her brother.

It felt weird, but it also felt good.

She got ready in record time. It wasn't even ten minutes before she came back down the stairs dressed in a pair of cut-off jean shorts and a white top. Her hair was still on top of her head, but it looked much more orderly than it did before.

She looked like a dream.

A dream I had way too many times to count, and for the first time in my life, I truly felt nervous to go on a date with someone.

"You look beautiful."

She smiled before tucking a nonexistent piece of hair behind her ear.

"Thanks. If I had known before, I would have dressed up or something."

"You're perfect, Livy."

Her shoulders relaxed a small bit and one of her hands toyed with the loose strings of her shorts. I wanted to be the one to do it. I wanted to touch every piece of her body. I wanted to explore every part of her that no one else got to see.

"So, where are we going?"

"It's a surprise." And she was going to love it.

...

When the bright lights of the bar sign came into view, she looked at me, confused. When I opened the door for her, she hesitated.

"I'm not going to be able to get in here, Parker."

"They don't ID at the door. Come on."

She grabbed my hand, climbing out of my truck, and we headed inside. It wasn't necessarily a bar, per se, more of a karaoke bar.

As soon as the lyrics to some Carrie Underwood song hit our ears at an alarmingly horrible octave, Livy's smile lit up her face.

I wanted to put that look on her face every single day.

"Are we going to sing?" She was already bouncing on her feet.

"Umm, no." I shook my head as I pulled out her chair that had a tear across the seat. "You are going to sing while I watch you."

"What?" She gave me a look that made my stomach tense up. "You have to sing with me, Parker. It will be so much fun." She batted her eyelashes.

"It's not happening." I chuckled. She could try to persuade

me all she wanted, but there was no way in hell that I was getting on that stage and singing in front of this group of strangers.

She let the idea drop as she started scrolling through the book looking for the perfect song to sing. She flipped the pages one by one, and her eyes roamed over all of her choices. Livy was always singing. In the car, at the lake, in her bedroom. She constantly had a song stuck in her head, and I think that most of the time she didn't even realize she was singing out loud.

But she did.

And I fucking loved it.

When she found the song, she quickly wrote her selection on a strip of white paper before folding it up.

"What are you going to sing?" I asked, genuinely curious.

"It's a surprise." She mirrored my words from earlier.

"You're really not going to tell me?"

"Nope," the word popped out of her mouth, "and you can turn those puppy dog eyes to someone else because they're not going to work."

I reached out for her hand but she held her arm in the air, far away from me.

"Livy," I smirked.

"Parker," she mocked.

I reached for the paper again, but she was too quick. All I managed to do was press my body against hers as I reached behind her for the paper. She was giggling, her body shaking against mine.

"Please." I looked down at her, her chest pressed against mine, her lips still in a perfect smile only a few inches away from mine.

"That's not fair, Parker." She put her hand on my chest, my heart racing beneath her touch.

"Life's not fair, Livy." I breathed out her name, but I

couldn't stand it anymore. I didn't give a shit what was on that piece of paper. I just wanted to touch her, to feel her, to taste her.

I leaned in another inch, her breath warm against my lips, but before I could close the gap, she slipped out from beneath me and handed the paper to the DJ.

Her eyes were clouded over, but she looked so damn happy, I couldn't even be mad at her for escaping me.

"You're right, Parker." She had her hand on her hip. "Life isn't fair. You better get ready to sing because it's show time." Her grin stretched so far across her face that her dimples popped out, and I wanted nothing more than to trace them with my tongue.

I opened my mouth to tell her there was no way in hell that I was getting on that stage, but I was interrupted by the DJ announcing our duet over the speakers.

I groaned and ran my hand down my face.

I didn't climb on the stage because I wanted to. I climbed on the stage because she was covering her mouth to stifle her laugh, and I wanted to be the one to put that look on her face every day.

I would give anything.

I was expecting her to have picked some sappy song to embarrass the hell of me, but it wasn't Livy's style. Instead, "Closer" by The Chainsmokers started playing through the speakers as she shoved a microphone in my hand.

"I don't know all the words," I whispered in her ear.

"They come up across the screen." She pointed to the little monitor in front of us, and I knew there was no way I was getting out of it.

So, I sang, and the more Livy got into it, so did I. She danced around the stage, singing the words without even glancing at the screen, and I watched her.

There was a small bead of sweat on the back of her neck that ran down her skin until it pooled against her shirt. She was on fire. Completely in her element, singing her heart out, and having a blast.

By the time we got off the stage, the bar was cheering, Livy was laughing, and I was falling so hard that I couldn't see straight.

CHAPTER 9

DON'T BE A PUSSY

LIV

PRESENT

I LOVED MY JOB. Granted, I had only worked here for three days so far, but it was an awesome three days.

Brandon was quite possibly one of the funniest people I had ever met, Parker was keeping his distance, and I had a major girl crush on Staci.

Staci was the only other tattoo artist in the shop, and she was by far the coolest chick I knew. Her hair was jet black and stick straight, and her creamy white skin was covered in bright, colorful tattoos.

She booked appointments nonstop, they all did actually, but she had a male clientele that didn't stop, and I couldn't blame them. She was gorgeous.

"You know it's sacrilegious to work in a tattoo shop and not have a tattoo, right?" She was sitting next to me behind the desk, thumbing through a magazine while waiting for her next appointment to show.

"It is not." I rolled my eyes. "It may be bad for business, but it's not sacrilegious."

"Why don't you get one?" She set down her magazine and

started looking over my skin as if she was looking for the perfect spot.

"I want to." I added another appointment into Parker's schedule. "It just makes me nervous."

Staci laughed, in a full on unattractive snort-laugh that made me like her more.

"Don't be a pussy, Liv."

"I am not being a pussy," I said the last word quietly which only made her laugh louder.

"What would you get?" She started looking around the walls at the artwork that was featured there for customers to choose from, but what I wanted wasn't on those walls. It was in a portfolio under my desk.

I had looked at the drawing every single day that I had worked there, and every single day, I wanted it more and more.

"I wouldn't get anything on the wall."

Staci looked at me like I was a bit crazy and maybe I was. I pulled the portfolio out and pointed to the drawing that I couldn't quit thinking about.

Wild at heart.

Staci whistled when she saw the drawing I was talking about before she put her feet up on the desk. "Good luck with that one."

"Why?" Typically if a client had requested a tattoo, it was pulled out of the portfolio. I didn't see anything that stated someone had claimed it.

"Because I've seen about a hundred people ask for that tattoo and the answer is always the same."

"Which is?"

"Nope." She clapped her hands theatrically, startling me a bit.

"Why?" I looked back down at the drawing. It was easily one of the best pieces of art I had ever seen.

"Because Parker won't let go of it. Someone always asks and he always says no."

"Well couldn't you tattoo it on me?" I batted my eyelashes at her, and she rolled hers.

"That," she pointed to my face, "doesn't work on me, and no, I can't. It's Parker's work. Only Parker can do it."

I thought about her words before sliding the drawing back in place. I loved it. Absolutely loved it, but there was no way in hell I was letting Parker tattoo me. It wasn't happening.

"Well then what good are you?" I teased, putting the portfolio back under the desk.

Staci's eyes lit up and the grin that took over her face scared me a bit.

"What is that look for?" I motioned toward her face as she had mine only moments before.

"How much time do we have before my next appointment?"

I looked at the appointment book. "Twenty minutes or so, why?"

"We should pierce something." She said it like most people don't take a day or two to think these things out. There was no hesitation or doubt.

"What?" I screeched.

"I already told you not to be a pussy, Liv. Let's do it!" She clapped her hands together like she just won the lottery, and I watched her like the crazy person she was.

"Your nose would be really cute." She turned my face this way and that. "Or even your lip. Or we could always." She held her hands over my chest and motioned like she was grabbing my tits.

"Wouldn't that hurt?" I rubbed my breasts just thinking about the pain.

"Only for a minute or so, but it's totally worth it." She winked at me.

"Do you have yours pierced?" I whispered even though we were the only two in the shop. Brandon and Parker left about an hour ago to run a few errands.

"Of course. I also have my hood pierced, and let me just tell you, I love that baby."

"Your vagina?" I shrieked.

"Yes. My vagina." She patted me on my head like a puppy. "Do you ever get laid, Liv?"

Her question was innocent, but she didn't realize how close to the truth she was because I wasn't getting laid. Not regularly. Not even semi-regularly. She would die if she knew it had been over a year, but I wasn't going to tell her that. Instead, I just shrugged my shoulders and let her question roll off me.

She shook her head as if the thought of not getting laid made her physically ill. "Okay. Let's start with the nipples."

My eyes widened. "Are you sure?"

"I'm positive. Live a little." I wasn't one for peer pressure, but I couldn't deny that the idea of having my nipples pierced excited me.

"This stays between us." I pointed my finger back and forth between us before Staci grabbed my hand and pulled me into her booth.

I watched her work, setting up her equipment, looking like a surgeon with all her sterile materials.

When it came time for me to take my top off, I only hesitated for a second. I was sitting in her chair naked from the waist up, and she was smiling at me like a loon.

"This is going to be perfect. You have a great set of tits."

I laughed and had the urge to cover my chest.

"Do you talk to all your clients like this?"

Staci shrugged. "No. Not all my clients have great tits.

Some come in here with tits to the floor and still want them pierced. Which is fine, to each their own, but it makes my day when I know someone down the road is really going to appreciate my work."

"You're insane." I gripped the edge of the chair as she made her way toward me with a clamp that looked like it was used to torture people.

"Maybe, but I know a great set of tits when I see one."

The metal bit down around my nipple, and I tensed, preparing myself for the pain.

"Will you stop talking about my tits?" I said through gritted teeth.

"Okay. Are you ever going to tell me about your history with Parker?"

Her question came out of left field and I wasn't expecting it, but before I could contemplate how to answer her, pain seared through my breast and my only thought was that this bitch lied.

That fucking hurt.

CHAPTER 10

LOSING CONTROL

LIV

FOUR YEARS AND FIVE AND A HALF MONTHS EARLIER

PEOPLE COME into our lives for a multitude of reasons. Some come for fleeting moments, some are there for a lifetime, and then there are those, the ones who it doesn't matter how long they are a part of your life. They make such an impact that a moment with them is more poignant than a lifetime with someone else.

That was what my moments with Parker were like.

When we finally walked out of the karaoke bar, my heart was racing, my shirt was damp with sweat, and my cheeks were hurting from smiling.

He pulled me to him when I leaned up against his truck, and I didn't think I had ever seen him smile so much.

"Those people in there think you're a rock star." He pointed over his shoulder toward the bar.

"Well I kind of am." I rolled my eyes dramatically.

"Uh huh." He chuckled and his hips pressed into mine. "I didn't know I was going to have to share you so much on our first date." He looked down at me, the flecks of gold in his green eyes shining in the neon lights.

"Well take me somewhere you don't have to share me," I whispered, my hands tightening in his t-shirt.

He pressed his forehead against mine before letting out a ragged breath.

"Let's go."

He pulled the door open and helped me into the truck. As soon as he climbed in, he lifted the console that separated us and patted the seat next to him. I had dreamed of riding in that spot forever, and when I finally settled in next to him, it felt like it was exactly where I belonged.

His hand rested on my knee, the warmth of his skin against mine was the best feeling in the world, and I watched his fingers trace circles against my skin while he drove.

I didn't know where he was taking me, and I didn't care. All that mattered was that I was with him in that moment and there was nothing anyone could do to ruin that.

We pulled up outside his grandfather's old house. I knew the place from coming out here a hundred times over the years, but we had never been here alone.

The property was pitch black, and I wouldn't have known where to step if it wasn't from memory. We walked around the back of the house wordlessly. Only the sound of our steps against the ground heard against the backdrop of the creek.

There were two old rocking chairs sitting in the back yard overlooking the water. They had been painted white at one point, but they had since chipped and peeled away, showing the years of use. Parker's grandparents use to sit out here and watch us play, but that was before his grandmother passed away and his grandfather went to a nursing home. Those rocking chairs had shared years of stories, laughter, and love.

The wood creaked under Parker's weight as he sat down. The house was beautiful, an older white farmhouse, but it was easy to see that his grandparents hadn't been able to take care of it over the years.

I sat down in the chair next to him pulling my knees to my chest.

"I love this place." He was looking out over the creek that ran along the back end of the property, and he looked so peaceful.

"I do too." I ran my finger over a piece of paint that was barely hanging on. "I used to love coming out here when we were kids."

"Yeah. That's because my grandparents spoiled you. They thought you hung the moon." His head was pressed against the back of the chair, and he turned it to face me, a lazy smile on his face.

"Who says I didn't?" He smiled bigger. "You can't blame them for loving me. I'm pretty awesome."

"No. I can't." He was staring at me, and every second his eyes were on me, I felt my breath leave my body. "He would love to see you, you know?"

"Who?" I tucked a piece of hair behind my ear that had fallen out of my bun.

"Papa. He asks about you all the time."

My chest ached as guilt filled it. Parker's grandfather was the closest thing I had to a real one, and it had been a long time since I went to see him. Too long.

"Let's go see him. Will you take me?"

"Of course." He nodded his head. "I planned on going tomorrow. Do you want to go with me?"

"Yeah." Plans. We were making plans. I told myself I wouldn't let myself get hopeful about whatever the hell we were doing, we were just going to see his papa, but it was impossible.

He stood from his chair before he reached for my hand. I

had no idea where he was taking me now, but I didn't care. He pulled his phone from his pocket and fiddled with it for a moment before music played from his speakers. Still gripping my hand, he pulled me closer to him and wrapped his other arm around my back.

"What are you doing?" I giggled.

"Well, I didn't really get to dance with you at the karaoke bar." He started moving against me causing my body to move with him.

"Okay?"

"I'm done missing out on things with you, so I'm dancing with you now."

He spun me around playfully before pulling me back against him, and I laughed, the sound getting lost in the trees that surrounded us.

"I never expected you to be this guy." I ran my hand up his chest before resting it behind his neck. I knew that Parker's girlfriends had loved him, but I never expected this. I had never seen this side of him before.

"I've never been this guy." He stared down at me, the moonlight illuminating his face, and I felt like I was in a dream.

It was all too good. Parker was too perfect. This night was too amazing.

"So why now?" I teased, feeling overwhelmed by the way he was looking at me.

"I think the better question is what took me so long." His words were muffled as he came closer to me, but I tasted them against my lips. I didn't realize how starved I was until that moment. Then his lips touched mine, the first drag of his lips stealing my breath.

I had thought about this moment forever, dreamed of it, wished for it, but I never imagined it would be this good.

His hands gripped in my hair angling me exactly where he

wanted me, and I gasped for breath as he pulled my bottom lip between his teeth.

His tongue ran along the same spot before it entered my mouth, and I only thought I was starving before.

We became a mess of lips, tongues, teeth, and hands. He gripped my waist in his hand before he pressed me against the house. I hadn't even realized we had moved, but I didn't care. I wrapped my legs around him, which seemed to shock him but only for a moment. He pressed into me, and I could feel him everywhere. I was surrounded by him, and I had never wanted to be somewhere so badly in my life.

My stomach was coiled tight, almost in pain, and I knew that I needed more from him. One of his hands was holding my weight under my ass while the other felt like a brand on my thigh. Searing me. Setting me on fire. I ran my hand against the edge of his t-shirt before running my fingers against the ridges of his stomach.

He shuddered under my touch, and I pressed my center into him harder, needing more.

His mouth pulled away from me, his forehead pressed against mine, but I wasn't ready to stop. I tried to bring his lips back to mine, but Parker took a step back, dropping me back to my feet.

I was leaning against the house, not trusting myself to hold my own weight yet, and he was staring at me, his hand running through his hair.

"Why'd you stop?" I asked, my voice breathless. My chest tight with anticipation of his answer.

"Because I'm about to lose every bit of control I have left." He took a deep breath. "Fuck, Livy." His gaze ran down my body, and I could feel it as if it was his hands. "Fuck."

CHAPTER 11

BROKEN PROMISES

PARKER

PRESENT

"WHAT DO you think about this one?" Emily held the fork out to me with another bite of cake on it. After fifteen different choices, they were all starting to blend together.

"It's good too."

"Ugh, Parker. We have to pick one. We don't have much time."

I wanted to tell her that we wouldn't be in this predicament if she hadn't fired the first baker, but I was smart enough to know that comment wouldn't be appreciated.

"Then I say lemon cake with that vanilla frosting." I pointed to the yellow cake that was getting lost in the sea of all the others.

"Really?" She snarled her lip. "I liked the chocolate one."

"Then get the chocolate one." I had to force myself not to roll my eyes. I didn't know why she brought me to this shit anyways. She didn't really care what my opinion was.

"Babe, I have to go. I have another appointment at one."

She smiled a tight smile, clearly irritated with me. "Okay. Love you."

"I love you too." I kissed her on the top of her head.

She didn't look back at me again as I walked out. Instead she was deep in conversation with the baker, pointing to the chocolate cake.

I pulled my phone out and checked the time. I only had about twenty minutes until my appointment, and I was grateful. I needed to get lost with the vibration of my gun in my hand. It would clear my head.

Livy didn't even look up when I walked into the door of the shop and that was fine. We had been pleasant toward each other since she started, having no problems, but we weren't friendly. I could hear her joking around and laughing with Brandon and Staci while I was in my station, which was great, but as soon as I entered the room she tensed up. She tried to hide it, but I could see it.

We could all see it.

I began setting up my equipment, the routine almost robotic. I had just got it set up when my client walked in the door. We shook hands, and I adjusted my chair for him.

Before I even had to ask her, Livy had my music playing through the speakers. I got to work on the massive back piece I was finishing. I had already spent about six hours on it about a month ago, doing all of the outline, and now he was back to have all the color work done.

An hour into it, I was completely zoned out and didn't even hear anyone else come into the shop. It wasn't until I heard Livy's voice and the words it was saying that my attention was pulled away from my work.

"I'm sorry. I already told you that we are completely booked out."

We were booked out pretty damn far, but not indefinitely.

"Seriously, Livy. I know Parker has something. You can't

refuse me an appointment." It was a woman's voice. It was vaguely familiar and slightly annoying.

"First, don't call me Livy. It's Liv. Second, we have the right to refuse service to anyone we want."

That got my attention.

"Give me a second," I said to my client, and he just nodded his head.

I poked my head around the door of my workspace to see who on earth Livy was being so rude to. We never refused to tattoo anyone unless they were underage, drunk, or just wanted something so incredibly stupid that I couldn't bring myself to tattoo it.

As soon as I saw the head of blonde hair that I knew belonged to my ex, Madison, I knew I might be in trouble. Livy was staring at her with murder in her eyes, and I didn't dare interrupt them. Madison stopped by the shop about once every six months. Every time she came by, I refused to see her, but it never seemed to deter her.

"You're a bitch, Liv." Madison sounded out her name.

"Yeah, well you're a fucking leech, Madison. Still trying to get close enough to suck the life out of him, huh? Didn't you hear he's getting married?" Livy was leaning over the desk precariously close to Madison.

"I did, actually." Madison swept her hair over her shoulder. "But I think the two of us have that in common, not giving a fuck if he's taken or not."

I could see the anger filling Livy, and I knew from experience that girl had quite a bit of fire inside her. When she burned, everyone else burned with her.

I needed to step in. I should have stepped in, but I also wanted to know Livy's reaction. I desperately wanted to know what was going on in that head of hers.

"That's where you're wrong, sweetheart," Livy spoke

through gritted teeth, looking hot as hell. "The only thing that the two of us have in common is that he broke both of our hearts. Now get the fuck out of here before I break something else."

Madison hesitated only a second before she turned on her heel and marched out the door, the chime echoing throughout the building. Livy pressed the heels of her hands against her eyes, and I knew she was trying to control herself. Trying to hide everything she was feeling in that moment.

She shook her hands out then her eyes met mine. She held my stare for a moment, giving away too much of herself, but not nearly enough. I wanted nothing more than to run to her and hold her against me. I wanted to tell her that she was nothing like Madison, that they didn't have a damn thing in common. There were so many things I wanted to tell her. So many things that were on the tip of my tongue, but I had a client lying in my chair, gloves on my hands, and a fiancée that I seemed to keep forgetting about when I was around her.

So instead of doing everything I wanted to, I reached for the control on the wall turning up the radio, then I went back to work trying to numb out everything that was running through my mind.

...

By the time I came up for air, it was dark outside and there was no one around. I rang my client up since Livy wasn't at her desk then shook his hand. He was a quiet guy. We barely spoke a handful of words during his session, but he was beyond happy with my work and that was all that mattered.

The door chimed as he walked out, and I wondered where in the hell everyone was. Staci's laugh rang out through the shop and I followed the sound into Brandon's workspace.

As soon as I saw them, rage filled me.

I had no right to feel that way.

It was insanity that I did, but it didn't change anything.

It rushed through my veins.

It took over every rational thought.

Livy was lying back in Brandon's chair, her shirt rolled up to the bottom of her breasts, her stomach completely on display.

I loved seeing the smooth skin of her stomach. It reminded me of times when we had gone swimming together, of the times I had her body under my touch, but then memories of her dancing half naked in front of my friends ran through my mind and seeing Brandon's hands on her now took every good memory I had and ruined them.

"What the hell are you doing?"

Livy looked up at me, confused. I didn't blame her. I was confused myself.

"I'm about to give Livy her first tattoo," Brandon said without looking up at me.

Staci was swiveling in a chair next to Livy, and she had a grin on her face that was often there. It was full of mischief.

"It's not happening."

Brandon's hands stopped pressing the transfer paper against Livy's skin, and he finally turned to look at me.

"I'm sorry. What?" Livy sat up, crumbling the design that rested against her body, making me smile.

I looked at her. Only at her. "If you want a tattoo, then I'll do it. Otherwise, it's not happening." I knew that I sounded like a maniac. Hell, I felt like one, but there was no way that I was allowing Brandon to ink her body. Not for her first time. Maybe not ever.

Just the thought of his hands running over her skin as he marked her for life was driving me insane.

Livy looked to Brandon for help maybe or advice. Either way, it pissed me off even more.

"Brandon?"

He didn't turn to look at her though. He was staring at me, watching me with his gaze that could see straight through me.

"It's cool, Liv," he said. "Let Parker do your first tattoo. Maybe he'll even do that drawing that you really wanted. You know the one, Parker? The heart with all the butterflies."

That motherfucker.

He knew what that drawing meant to me. He knew why I had always refused to tattoo it on anyone.

It reminded me of Livy. I think subconsciously, I drew it for her.

"Parker James," Livy stood, pulling down her shirt. "You piss me the fuck off."

She stormed out of the room, knocking into my chest on her way out the door. Brandon and Staci both tried to stifle their laugh so I flipped them the bird before I walked out, following her.

"You piss me off too, Livy."

She stopped in her tracks, her hand resting on the desk, and her chest heaving in anger.

"What the hell did I do to piss you off?" She turned toward me.

"You knew that I'd be mad if you let Brandon tattoo you. Is that why you did it? To get under my skin?"

She narrowed her eyes at me. "Why would I want under your skin, Parker?"

"I don't know." I ran my fingers through my hair. "But you promised me that I would be the first person to ever tattoo you."

It was a stupid thing to say. Did she promise me that? Yes. Was that a long ass time ago? Yes again.

"Are you kidding me? That was over four years ago. Four

fucking years." She held up four fingers for emphasis. "And you promised me way more than that, buddy. I guess it's my turn to start breaking some promises."

Her words hit their mark, exactly where she intended for them to, and I felt it burn in my chest.

She pulled her bag from underneath her desk then looked up at me again. "I'm going home for the night."

"Okay," I said hesitantly.

"I wasn't asking for permission." She gave me an evil look, and I wanted to close the few steps that were separating us. I wanted to kiss the attitude right out of her. I wanted to apologize for everything I had ever done to her with the touch of my lips, and I wanted to punish her for still making me want her with the force of my tongue and the nip of my teeth.

But instead, I let her walk out, and I had no clue what I was thinking.

CHAPTER 12

BINGO

PARKER

FOUR YEARS AND FIVE AND A HALF MONTHS EARLIER

I HATED the smell of nursing homes. As soon as the smell hit me, it made me feel depressed and lonely, but my hand was resting in Livy's as we walked toward my grandfather's room.

"Hey, Papa," I called out as soon as we walked in the door.

It smelled different in his room. The scent of tobacco and leather filled the air, and it reminded me of all the time I had spent with this man.

"Well I'll be damned if it isn't my Livy." He was sitting in a chair in the corner of the room, and he looked happy.

"Hey, Papa." She waved, but he wasn't having any of that.

"Girl, get your ass over here and give me some love."

She giggled as she made her way to him, and he pulled her into his arms. His grip was a lot weaker than it used to be, but I could see him cling to her with everything he had.

She sat down in the chair next to him, and he gripped her hand in his.

"How are you, Livy?"

"I'm really good." She smiled at him. "How are you?"

"Oh, I'm living the dream." He lifted his free hand in the

air and motioned around the room. "I have all this, plus some good-looking nurses who take care of me, and I'm the reigning champion of bingo."

She laughed at his antics, and he smiled at her, a broad smile that could never be faked. That was the thing about Papa. He was always genuine, and he always made everyone happier just by being around him.

"Ummm... Hi, Papa." I waved at him from his bed, and Papa rolled his eyes.

"Oh, hi, Parker." He rolled his eyes playfully. "I'm so glad you're here. You're my favorite grandson in the world."

"He's my only grandson," Papa mock-whispered to Livy.

"Don't get jealous, boy. You know I love you, but it's not every day that I get to see my Livy. Plus, she's much prettier than you to look at." Papa winked at her, and I groaned. "Don't groan at me. I saw you holding her hand when you walked in. What's going on there?"

Livy started to pull her hand from Papa's, but Papa's grip held firm. I saw him give her hand a squeeze for reassurance as they waited for me to reply.

"Papa." I ran my hand over my face. "We're hanging out." My eyes met hers.

"What the hell does that mean? You two always hang out."

"Well now we're hanging out without Mason around." I looked at my grandfather trying to get him to read between the lines.

"Oh, so you like my Livy." Papa wagged his eyebrows at me, and Livy snorted out a laugh.

"Yes, Papa. I like her." My voice was soft, and Livy looked up at me with a soft smile on her face.

I more than liked her.

"It's about damn time." Papa stood from his chair pulling

Livy with him. "Well come on, lovebirds. Bingo starts in five minutes."

I followed them down the hall. He stopped every few feet to introduce Livy to anyone he saw, bragging on how beautiful she was, and she couldn't stop smiling.

We spent the next few hours playing bingo with Papa, him winning every time, and laughter filling the air.

"I'm sorry I had to beat you Livy," he whispered in her ear, "but I couldn't let George think I was getting soft."

"It's okay, Papa. I wouldn't want to ruin your reputation."

He winked at her before turning back to his bingo board. It was so easy to see how much he loved Livy, and it made me wonder if everyone could see through me so easily.

I pulled her into me and kissed her softly against her lips.

"Thank you," I said against her neck.

"For what?" she said breathlessly.

"For being you."

CHAPTER 13

NO BITCHING

LIV

PRESENT

BROKEN HEARTS AREN'T the worst thing in the world. Having a broken heart and getting a reminder of how broken it was daily? That fucking sucked.

I thought I could handle it. I didn't think I would be so affected after all this time, but every day when his phone rang, I held my breath to see if he would say I love you before hanging up.

As much as it hurt me, I needed to get closer to him. I needed some sort of connection. I knew how bad of an idea that was. I didn't need someone to tell me how idiotic I was being. I had already told myself. But a broken heart was the worst listener in the world, and all that bitch could see was him. She didn't care about anything else. It is easy to swallow down the lies when your heart is hungry.

It had been three days since the incident with Brandon. I was so pissed off when he refused to allow Brandon to tattoo me. He acted like he was my father. He acted like he had some right to tell me what to do.

But as pissed as I was, the thought that kept running

through my brain on repeat was that he cared. That little bloom of, I don't know, hope maybe? Poison? Either way, it weaseled its way into my chest and sank its teeth into me. I couldn't get it out of my mind.

I knew that it shouldn't have mattered if he cared, but no matter how much I tried to lie to myself, it did.

Parker had just finished tattooing a portrait of a man's daughter on his arm. It was beautiful, life-like, and so damn impressive. I knew from our past that he was talented. I had spent many hours sitting around watching him draw. But what he did now? It was beyond anything that I could imagine.

I looked at the clock. Four fifty-six. Fuck. My fingers tapped against the desk, and I tried to keep my foot from bouncing against my chair.

Parker walked out from his workspace. He was wearing a simple white t-shirt and jeans, and it was unfair how damn hot he was. The crisp white of his shirt seemed to make the colors of his tattoos pop even more than normal, and his eyes. God. His eyes.

"Is my next appointment here yet?" He leaned against my desk, his arms crossed below him.

"Yep." I avoided his eyes.

He turned his head to look out in the waiting room then looked back at me.

"Are they in the bathroom?" he asked curiously.

"Nope."

"Okay," he said hesitantly. "Want to clue me in?" He chuckled softly.

I set his drawing down in front of him. The one I loved. The one he refused to tattoo on anyone.

He looked down at the drawing, stared at it for a moment before his gaze returned to mine. He didn't say anything. He just watched me. He watched me in a way that I knew he saw too much. He always had.

"I'll make you a deal." I put my face on my fist, leaning in for dramatic affect. "I'll let you do my first tattoo if you do this." I pointed down at the drawing that lay between us.

He continued to stare at me, but his gaze dropped from my eyes to my lips. My breath caught in my throat, and it seemed to snap him out of it.

"Deal." He stood to his full height and held the drawing in his hand.

"Really?" I squeaked. I had expected him to put up at least a bit of a fight after the things Brandon and Staci had told me about the drawing.

"Yes, really. Now come on." He started walking toward his workspace, and I hopped out of my chair to follow him.

I climbed into his chair while he started pulling things out of drawers and setting everything up. I didn't know what half the crap was, but I trusted him. By the time he rolled his stool up next to me with black gloves covering his hands, the only thought that was crossing my mind was that he was about to touch me.

"Where are we doing it?" He held a stencil in his hand. The drawing ready to transfer to my skin.

"I was thinking over my ribs." I pointed to the right side of my body.

"Bold choice. You know they are one of the most painful spots, right?"

"I can handle it." I shrugged my shoulders.

"Okay." He grinned. "But I don't want to hear any bitching."

I smacked him on his arm, and he laughed softly before he started rolling up my shirt. The muscles of my stomach tightened under his touch. He leaned my chair back until I was completely stretched out in front of him. He finished rolling my shirt up and tucked it precariously under my bra.

Chill bumps covered my skin as he cleaned it with his damp paper towel. When his fingers pressed the stencil against my skin, I held my breath and tried not to squirm under his touch.

"Do you want to make sure it's right?" he asked as he leaned back to look at the stencil. He examined it from several different angles, making sure it was perfect.

"No. I trust you." I didn't think about the words until after I said them, but I couldn't take them back. I watched Parker swallow down my words, the movement of his throat mesmerizing.

"You ready?"

I looked up at him, his gun in his hand, and my heart in my throat. "Yeah. I'm ready."

Then the pain started. I tried to hold as still as I possibly could, but there were moments when Parker would push down on my hip to keep me in place. He wiped the ink from my skin, rubbed some sort of salve over the work he had already done, and then he continued working. He looked so serious as he concentrated on his gun against my skin. His brow was furrowed, and he constantly pulled his bottom lip in between his teeth. I wanted his lips against mine, I wanted his teeth against my body, and I felt like I was about to lose my mind.

"Are you okay?" He ran his paper towel over my skin again, collecting the excess ink.

"Yeah. Why?" I ran my hand through my hair.

"Your stomach is trembling." He was watching me, waiting for my response.

"Oh." I tightened my stomach muscles. I hadn't even realized it was happening.

"Why don't we take a break?" He pulled his gloves off. "I've got the outline finished."

"Can I look at it?" I leaned over trying to see my ribs, but Parker caught my chin in his hand, stopping me.

"Not happening." We stared at each other, my face in his hand, my pulse racing. His eyes seemed glazed over as he looked at me, and when his thumb ran over my bottom lip softly, I knew we were in dangerous territory.

"Parker." His name was a whisper on my lips, the taste of memories and pain and the desire for something I knew was wrong for me. Something that was wrong for both of us.

He pulled his thumb away from me, leaving a trail of fire and want behind. "I'm going to go get some fresh air." He stood from his stool, the legs hitting the wall, before taking a deep breath and walking out.

I stood from my chair, careful not to touch my new tattoo, and I went to Staci's room. She was lying back in her chair with a piece of paper over her face, and I couldn't tell if she was sleeping or not.

I pushed on her foot, and she slowly sat up, blinking.

"Were you napping?" I sat down on her stool.

"Me? Nope. Never. I would never nap at work." She was grinning a shit-eating grin, and I came to realize that was her normal look.

"Uh huh."

"Holy shit." She sat up further in her chair.

"What?" I looked around the room, confused.

"He did it." She pointed down at my tattoo. "He really fucking did it."

I was worried that maybe he had tattooed something crazy on me instead of doing the drawing I asked for, but I still avoided looking down at it. Well, because he told me to.

"What did he do?" I asked hesitantly.

"Motherfucker." She stood up and paced in her small space.

"What's wrong?" I started to look down at the tattoo because you know, that shit is for life.

"He actually tattooed that drawing on you." She pointed to my ribs again. "Do you know how many people he's said no to?"

I shook my head, but she wasn't finished.

"Me either because it's more than I could count. I thought this was a sure thing. That asshole. Now I'm out a hundred dollars."

"Umm, Staci. You're confusing the hell out of me."

"That tattoo. I made a bet with Brandon that Parker wouldn't do it." She narrowed her eyes on me. "Brandon must know something that I don't know. Spill it."

"Not here." I looked out her door to see Parker coming back inside.

"Tonight." She pointed at me. "We're going out when he's finished with you."

She didn't realize how much her words would affect me, but she also didn't know that Parker had been finished with me long before tonight. If we were all going to work together, I might as well tell her. God knows that Parker had already told Brandon what went down between us.

"Deal."

She grinned again as I walked out of her room and headed back to Parker.

"You ready to finish up?" I climbed back into his chair. He was sitting on his stool and his head was buried in his phone.

"Yea."

He put his phone in his pocket. "This might be brutal though. The outline is already trying to heal and when I go over it with fresh ink, it might hurt like a bitch."

"I can handle it." But I wasn't sure that I could because he was right. The first time hurt, but ripping open my wounds with fresh pain was likely to kill me.

"Okay. Let me know if he becomes too much." He pressed his gun against my ribs again, this time the pain more intense than the last.

CHAPTER 14

TRUTH OR DARE

LIV

FOUR YEARS AND FIVE MONTHS EARLIER

Four Years and five months earlier

PARKER and I were either being really careful, or my brother didn't pay very good attention. Actually, the only thing he seemed to pay attention to these days was all the girls he had coming in and out of his rotating door.

It had been two weeks since Parker had taken me to the karaoke bar, and it had been the best two weeks of my life. We had gone to dinner, to the movies, to the mountains, but we hadn't even come close to getting as physical as we had the night at his grandparents.

I didn't know why either. It wasn't from a lack of trying on my part. Every time I thought something was going to happen, he would change the subject, move away from me, or pretend like he didn't notice.

But tonight wasn't up to him. I was making the plans, and he didn't have a choice.

When I pulled up outside his house, one hour before our plans, I sent him a text.

I hope you don't have any plans tonight.

Parker: ??? I have plans with you. Don't I?

You do! Get your butt outside.

A MOMENT LATER, he poked his head out the door and looked out at me standing with my back against my car. I was wearing a pair of cut-off blue jean shorts that I knew drove him crazy, a tied up white tank top, and a pair of aviator sunglasses. He walked up to me slowly, his gaze running from my head to my toes.

"What's all this about?" He put his hand on my hip pulling my body close to his.

"Change of plans." He watched my lips as I spoke. "We're not going to the movies tonight."

"Oh yeah? Then what are we doing?"

"It's a surprise." I pushed him away from me with my hands on his chest and pointed to the passenger seat. "Now get in."

He grinned before climbing into my car, and as soon as I took my seat behind the wheel, he pulled my hand to his and kissed my knuckles.

After thirty minutes of holding my hand and trying to guess where we were going, he finally asked, "Are you really not going to tell me where we're going?"

"Nope. What kind of surprise would that be?"

He huffed and looked out the window.

It was ten minutes later when we pulled up to an old campground that my mom used to bring my brother and me to before she forgot to give a shit anymore.

"What are we doing?" He stepped out of the car and looked around at the nothingness that was before us.

I popped the trunk of my car, which was packed to the brim with camping gear. "We're going camping."

He looked into my trunk and then back at me. "And your brother? Where does he think you're going to be tonight?"

I pulled him closer to me, my finger in his belt loop. "At a friend's house. Tonight it's just you and me."

...

The tent was set up, sleeping bags laid out, fire going, and Parker seemed to be keeping a wide berth from me.

There was hesitation in his eyes that I had frequently seen over the last couple weeks. He was nervous to be alone with me. I didn't know his reasoning, but he didn't have a choice tonight. There was no one else around. Not for miles.

"Do you want to play a game?" I sat down in a chair next to the fire, and he sat down directly across from me.

"What kind of game?" he asked hesitantly, but the smirk that caused me to fall in love with him pulled at his lips.

"Truth or dare?" I shrugged.

"Okay." He took a sip of his water and I watched his throat as he swallowed.

"I'll go first." I leaned forward in my seat and watched him. "Truth or dare, Parker?"

"Truth." He grinned.

"Did I mention that if you refuse to tell the truth or complete your dare you have to strip?"

"You can't make up rules as we go." He moved closer to the fire, matching me.

"I do what I want, Parker James. Now tell the truth. How many girls have you been with?"

He stared me down before pulling his black t-shirt over his head. A small pang of jealousy hit my chest, but I knew he wouldn't answer the question. And I couldn't be jealous when I was the one who got to sit across from him without his shirt on.

"So we're going to play dirty, huh?" He raised his eyebrow. "Truth or dare?"

I tapped on my chin as if it was the hardest decision I had ever made. "Dare."

He narrowed his eyes. He hadn't expected me to pick dare, but he should have learned a long time ago that I would never back down from a challenge.

"I dare you to kiss me."

I stood from my chair and made my way over to him. He angled his face toward me, but instead of kissing him, I took the opportunity to lower myself down, straddling his lap.

"What are you doing?" His hands gripped my hips as if I was about to attack him.

"Kissing you. That was my dare wasn't it." I leaned my body into his and ran my tongue over his neck where I could see his pulse.

"Livy," he growled.

"Yes?" The word was a whisper on my lips as I sucked his earlobe into my mouth.

"You're not playing fair." He gripped my hips harder.

I leaned back to look at him. "You weren't specific about the kiss, and you can't make up rules as we go." I winked at him, and he rolled his eyes. "Truth or dare?"

"Dare."

"I dare you to close your eyes for ten seconds and during those ten seconds you can't stop whatever it is I'm doing?"

He swallowed, hard. "If I refuse?"

"Then these bad boys are coming off." I pulled on the leg of his jeans before he bit out a curse.

He leaned his head against the back of the chair and his eyes slowly slid closed. The muscles of his abs were tightened in anticipation, and they jumped under my touch as I ran my hand over the ridges of muscle.

I pressed my lips to the corner of his and his hands bit into my hips as I ground down against him. I ran my mouth down his neck, peppering kisses against his skin, and causing goosebumps with a trail of my teeth.

"Truth or dare?" His voice was rough and my thighs involuntary tightened against him.

"Truth." I ran my tongue against his collarbone.

"What the hell do you think you're doing?"

I leaned back away from him then I slowly lifted my shirt from my body.

"What are you doing?" he whispered as if we were about to be caught.

"That's more than one question, but I didn't feel like answering the first so I'm paying the consequences."

He ran his hand through his hair, but his gaze stayed glued to my breasts. "We can't do this, Livy."

He didn't look like he believed what he was saying. He looked like this was exactly what he wanted to do.

"Truth or dare?"

He looked up at my face, then. Lust staring back at me.

"Truth."

"Why don't you want me?"

"What?" He stood from the chair, me in his arms.

"You heard me."

He was walking, and I had no idea where he was taking us. I couldn't take my eyes away from him. We crashed into the tent, his body falling on top of me, his weight supported by his arms.

"Don't say that shit again, Livy." His voice was stern, and I didn't push him. "I have never wanted something so bad in my life." He ran his nose along my chest, his skin brushing against the skin of my breast. "But you are worth more."

He started to pull away from me, but I wrapped my legs around his waist and held him against me.

"Don't say that again." He watched me. His eyes searching my face. "I want you to be my first, Parker. I want you to be my last. Please don't make me beg you."

I barely finished my sentence before his mouth slammed against mine. It wasn't a kiss like you see in the movies where our mouths moved perfectly against each other as we tasted each other. Instead, our kiss was desperate. He drug my bottom lip through his teeth and my hips rose to meet his, begging for more. His hands were wrapped in my hair and our chests heaved against one another.

He pulled his mouth away from mine and I groaned at the loss. But then his tongue tasted my neck and I had never wanted it anywhere more.

I gripped his hair in my hands as he moved his way down my body. The air hit my breasts as he pulled the cups of my bra down. He looked down at me, admiring my body, and I squirmed under his stare.

"You are so fucking beautiful." He laid his hand at the base of my neck before running it down my chest and cupping my breast in his hand.

His eyes held mine as he lowered his mouth, watching me, teasing me, and when his tongue met my nipple, I almost came out of my skin. He took his time with me, my stomach clenched tight and my panties soaked by the time he popped the button of my jean shorts.

"Are you sure?" He stared into my eyes, and I knew in that moment that regardless where we went from here, this moment would always be one of the most real moments I would ever know. We were raw and sure and completely in love.

"I've never been surer of anything in my life."

He pressed his forehead against mine, his breath harsh against my lips.

He slowly pulled my shorts down my legs followed by my panties. He was taking his time and touching every inch of my skin.

He kissed his way up my legs, and my stomach tightened as he pushed my thighs apart. My legs shook under his touch. My heart raced under his stare.

He watched me, never moving his gaze from mine, as he lowered his mouth between my thighs. My back arched as he pressed his lips against me, and I gripped his shoulders when his tongue tasted me for the first time.

I had never experienced anything like it in my life. I had never felt so exposed, so worshiped, or so needy.

He took his time until I was a writhing mess underneath him, and by the time he moved up my body, I felt like I was going to come out of my skin. He lined himself up against me, and I arched my body begging him for more.

But he didn't move.

He just stared down at me, watching me, and driving me crazy.

"Please, Parker," I begged, desperate for him.

He ran his hand against my forehead moving my hair out of my face before pushing into me slowly. The pain was instant and overwhelming, but I didn't have time to think about it because his mouth was next to my ear and he was whispering words that I never thought I'd hear.

"I love you, Olivia."

"Parker." His name was a cry on my lips.

"I do. I fucking love you." He began moving inside me

slowly, careful not to hurt me.

"I love you too."

He pressed his mouth to mine then he took his time worshipping my body. We clung to each other like it was the only moment we had, and we whispered each other's names as he brought me to the brink.

But we didn't worry about my brother.

We didn't worry about what anyone else would think.

We didn't worry about his past or mine or what tomorrow would bring.

The only thing I could see in my future was him.

...

Parker and Mason were in my living room when I walked in the door from school. I tried not to get giddy when I saw Parker sitting there, but he winked at me when Mason wasn't looking and I couldn't stop.

"How was school?" Mason asked.

"Boring. I'm so ready for it to be over." I threw my backpack on the ground, and Parker nodded toward the kitchen.

I made my way to the kitchen and grabbed a soda from the refrigerator. When I closed the refrigerator door, Parker pinned me against it and pressed his lips against mine.

"What are you doing?" I whispered while I looked over his shoulder for my brother.

"I couldn't stand not touching you for another second," he murmured against my skin as he ran his nose up my neck.

"You're going to get us caught." I leaned my head back against the refrigerator and gave him better access.

He nipped on my earlobe, causing me to moan softly before he started kissing my neck. "Tell me to stop," he whispered in my ear.

I couldn't tell him to stop, and he knew it. I had absolutely no will power when it came to him.

I clutched his t-shirt in my hands and pressed my hips against his. He wrapped one arm around my back and his other trailed over my stomach.

I didn't tell him to stop when his hand cupped my breast over my shirt, and I didn't tell him to stop when his hand slid under my jeans.

I pressed my face into his shoulder when his finger ran over my clit. He was gentle and soft and slow, and it was driving me crazy.

My hands dug into him as I felt my orgasm building. There was something so risky and thrilling about sneaking around behind my brother's back. I knew I should have at least felt somewhat guilty, but instead I felt a rush over the possibility of being caught.

My legs shook as Parker moved his finger faster and faster against me, and when he entered a finger inside me, I completely fell apart.

He slammed his mouth over mine to catch my moans, and I bit down on his lip as my orgasm racked through me.

"Hey, Parker," my brother called from the other room, and I tensed as the last waves of pleasure ran through me.

"Yeah?" Parker called back to him while staring into my eyes.

"Grab me a soda. Will you?"

Parker smirked before pressing another kiss to my lips. He stared at me as he put his finger into his mouth and before slowly pulling it back out.

I watched him, my legs still trembling from his touch, and my heart still racing from the rush.

He grabbed my soda off the counter, kissed me one more time, then walked out into the living room to my brother.

CHAPTER 15

WILD AT HEART

PARKER

PRESENT

HER CHEST WAS RISING and falling quickly as she tried to breathe through the pain. Normally, I didn't really care if it was hurting while I was tattooing, but with her, I cared about everything.

I wiped over my work, gathering the excess ink, and ran my finger over her skin. I watched as her stomach shuddered under my touch. Her shirt was tucked underneath her bra, pulling it tight against her breast, and her stomach was completely exposed. The curve of her hip vastly different from all the hard edges that surrounded her.

That was the thing about Livy, she always stood out from everything else. When everyone else was being serious, she would have a spark of mischief in her eyes. When everyone else was quiet, she always had something to say.

That was the reason I did this tattoo for her, the reason I drew it for her. She had been born wild. She was fierce, she was crazy, she was funny, but most of all, she was unpredictable. She never took the road that most traveled upon, and she surprised me at every turn.

She was chaos and madness, her heart never sitting still for long, and when I was with her, everything else crumbled away and I felt like I was home.

"Why was she here?" I looked up at her, but she had her eyes covered with her arm.

"Who?" I rubbed some salve over her fresh ink.

"Come on, Parker." She huffed causing her full pink lips to pout. "Madison."

"She shows up here about once every six months or so."

She moved her arm, finally giving me her eyes.

"What does she want?"

"What does Madison always want? To stir up shit. She thinks if she keeps coming here that I'll eventually tattoo her and that it will spark something between us, but it won't. I always refuse anyway."

She looked away from me slightly, and I knew she was thinking about the other day when she sent her away.

"She seemed pissed that you were here though."

"You caught that?" She winced.

"Yup. I watched the whole thing." I chuckled softly.

"Well thanks a lot. You could have come out there and helped me, you know."

"That's true, but then I wouldn't have been able to watch you go all territorial over me." I grinned.

No matter what she said and no matter how different our lives had become, she still cared.

"Please." She rolled her eyes. "I just didn't want to look at her for any longer than I had to."

"Uh huh." I stripped my gloves off my hands and reached my hand out to her. She looked at it suspiciously and regret filled my chest. There was a time when Livy would take my hand without question. She had trusted me fully, and I ruined that.

"We're all done." I motioned to her new ink, and she smiled. It was a smile that made me question everything. Emily was safe. She was the exact opposite from Livy, but in that moment, being safe terrified me more. I needed to know that I would taste the chaos again, and even though Livy's fire scared the shit out of me, I had more fear of never again feeling her burn.

She took my hand hesitantly, and I pulled her out of my chair and close to me.

"Are you ready?" She was only a few inches away from me, and I couldn't take my eyes off the curve of her lips.

"For what?" She looked like my Livy in that moment. She looked like she was up for anything. The rebellious girl I knew shining through.

"To see your tattoo."

"Of course." A smile lit up her face, the moment gone in a flash.

She moved in front of the mirror, and she gasped as she took in her ink. It fit her so perfectly. The size was perfect over her ribs, the colors beautiful against her skin tone, and most of all, the wild, wicked heart, a perfect representation of her own.

"I fucking love it." She turned this way and that in the mirror watching the way the ink moved as her body did. I watched her looking at herself, mesmerized by her own body, mesmerized by my art.

"Thank you so much, Parker." Her eyes met mine in the mirror. "I know that this drawing must have meant something to you because you have turned down so many people. Thank you for doing it for me."

"You're welcome." I hesitated. I didn't know how much to tell her. I didn't know if I could face telling her the truth, but it also felt wrong to lie to her. "Livy, I..." I rubbed my hand down the back of my neck. "I drew that for you."

She looked back down at the tattoo, her eyes bouncing around the artwork. She didn't say anything. She just stared. The butterflies fluttered against her skin as her chest rose and fell rapidly.

Her finger traced around the tattoo, careful not to touch the fresh ink. "Why?" Her voice was barely a whisper.

I thought about how to answer her. I wasn't sure if she was ready to hear the whole truth. I didn't think either one of us were ready to face it.

"Because it's you." I shrugged. "I was so mad at you when you left. Fuck. I was furious."

She was staring at me in the mirror, her eyes not leaving mine for a second.

"I got so into my art after that. I spent all my days and nights drawing."

"And this?" She looked so vulnerable, so fragile, so unlike herself.

"That is you." I pointed down to her ribs. "You have always been so wild at heart. Like a wildfire that can never be tamed. That's why I had to let you go."

She closed her eyes, blocking her against my words. Shielding her.

"That's bullshit, Parker, and you know it."

When she opened her eyes again, there was fire there. Pure and uncontrollable, and even though I should have been worried about her anger, I fed off her passion.

"You were eighteen years old. Your life was just starting. What did you want me to do? Get you stuck here with me?"

Finally, she turned toward me. "I wouldn't have been stuck. I would have chosen you." She was furious, her voice rising, but I didn't give a fuck if anyone else heard us. "But you didn't give me a choice."

"I know, Livy." My heart was beating against my chest causing my ribs to ache. I felt like I was there again, like I was about to lose her, but I didn't see any other option. "But neither did you."

CHAPTER 16

THE BOMB

PARKER

FOUR YEARS AND FIVE MONTHS EARLIER

Four years and five months earlier

I FELT like I was high. It was that insane rush of adrenaline, the blissful high, and the untouchable happiness.

Nothing could touch us. Nothing could bring us down. Or at least I thought.

We had been spending all of our time together. Typically I felt suffocated when I spent too much time with a girl.

With Livy, it was different. With her, it was everything.

I had just gotten home only a few hours ago, but already I was itching to be around her again. I felt off when I wasn't around her. I almost felt lost.

But I was supposed to be spending the day with Mason today. I had been neglecting him, and I didn't want him to become suspicious of me and his sister. Because it would ruin everything.

I was lying down on my couch when there was a loud knock on the door. I hesitated for a moment if I actually wanted to lift my feet and stand up because Mason never knocked, ever. But the thought that it may be Livy at the door got me to move my ass.

As soon as I saw her blonde hair through the glass panes of the door, I regretted my decision. I would have turned around too if she hadn't seen me as well. Instead, I begrudgingly cracked the door open and leaned against the frame.

Madison stood in front of me, and she didn't look like herself. The usually over-confident girl looked worried and nervous. Her eyes were puffy and her bottom lip trembled, but for the life of me, I couldn't feel sorry for her. Instead, I watched her, waiting for the Madison bomb to go off.

"Can I come inside?" She looked behind her as if she was worried someone would see her.

"What do you want, Madison?" I closed my eyes and counted to five. I didn't know how I ever dated this girl. Was I that big of an idiot?

"I need to talk to you. Please, Parker."

Running my hand down my face, I knew it was a bad idea, but I opened the door anyways.

She walked into my space like she knew it, and I guess she did. She took a seat on the couch, in the same spot where I was just sitting, and I sat in the chair across from her. I didn't ask her what she wanted again, I just waited for her to speak. There was something about her that made me feel uneasy.

"I don't know how to tell you this." She bit her bottom lip between her teeth which I would have thought was sexy once upon a time, but I didn't trust it anymore.

"Just say it." I wasn't up for her bullshit games.

"I'm pregnant, Parker." Her hand flew out to me and gripped tightly between her fingers rested a black and white photograph.

Her words hit me like a ton of bricks, crushing my chest, and making it impossible to breathe. I ripped the photo out of her hand, and I studied it. Looking for something that would make sense. There were white lines all over the image, but I couldn't tell what was what.

"What?" My voice was shaking along with everything else.

"I wanted to wait to tell you until I was sure. I went to the doctor this morning, but when I came by here, you were gone."

That's because I was with Livy. Fuck. Livy. This would destroy us. This would ruin everything. I stared at her stomach and watched as she ran her hand over it calmly.

I'd be lying if I said that I wasn't scared shitless because I was, but I was also mad at myself. I was furious that I had been so stupid, but we had used protection every time. Every. Single. Time.

I didn't know how this could happen. My mom was going to kill me. I remembered what she had said about what mine and Madison's child would look like. I could imagine the disappointment in her eyes. I could feel it in my chest.

"What do we do?" My hair was in my hands and my heart was in my throat.

Madison just smiled at me, a sweet smile that didn't belong on her face, and my whole world fell apart.

CHAPTER 17

COCK BLOCKED

LIV

PRESENT

THIS WAS A BAD IDEA.

I knew it as soon as I zipped up my bag.

Apparently, it was a yearly thing. A tattoo convention in South Carolina that Forbidden Ink attended every year, and this year, I was a part of the shop.

Brandon put my bag in the back of his SUV as Staci piled into the back seat with a pillow and a blanket.

"Are you sure there's enough room?" I asked Brandon for the third time. "I don't care to drive."

"You're riding with us, Liv. Get over it." He tugged on my side braid before climbing into the passenger's seat.

I blew out a deep breath as I watched Parker kissing Emily goodbye. She clung to him like she was desperate for him not to go, and although I could sympathize with the feeling, I had the urge to grab her by her hair and pull her off him.

When Parker climbed into the driver's seat, I tried my hardest to avoid his eyes. We had become civil over the last week, but I couldn't stand to look at him after he had just been with her. I knew how irrational that was. He was hers. He was about to marry her. I told myself and my heart that we had no business caring about him, no business wanting him, but neither of us listened.

"Girls get to pick the music," Staci yelled before jumping in between the front seats to grab Parker's phone that was already connected.

"Not happening." Parker tried to grab his phone from her, but she was too quick.

I laughed as Staci flipped him off before she started scrolling through his phone.

"Holy shit." Staci's voice was barely a whisper, but I heard it before one of my favorite songs from high school started playing through the speakers.

"Damn it, Staci." Parker grabbed his phone out of her hands, and she let him. But not before I saw it. Before I saw the words across the screen.

Livy's Playlist.

My eyes met his in the rearview mirror, the look on his face crushing me, but he quickly looked away. He stopped the song before it even got to the good part and a song I didn't even recognize started blaring through the car.

As Parker pulled out onto the highway, Staci nudged my arm.

"Holy shit," she mouthed to me.

I couldn't take it. The urge to ask Parker what the hell that was about, to ask him what he sees in her. But none of it was fair. Not to him or to me. So, instead of torturing either of us, I buried my face in my pillow and prayed that I could sleep for most of the drive.

...

"You're an idiot," I could hear Brandon's voice, but I wasn't sure where it was coming from.

"Fuck you too." Parker sounded irritated.

I turned my head out of my pillow to look at them. Staci was passed out with her head in my lap, and Brandon looked serious.

He was about to open his mouth to say something else, but then his gaze caught me and he stopped.

"Hey, Liv."

"Hey." I stretched my arms over my head. "Where are we?"

I looked out my window, but the rows of trees that passed us by weren't much help. I rolled down my window a bit, and I could smell salt water in the air.

"We're almost there," Parker said while watching me in his mirror. "We've got about ten more minutes."

When we pulled up to the hotel, I poked Staci in her boobs to wake her up. When it didn't work, I poked her again.

She scared the shit out of me when she snatched my finger without even opening an eye. "Don't start something you aren't willing to finish, Liv."

She popped her eyes open and grinned at me.

"All I did was poke your boob. Are you that hard up?" I laughed.

"The opposite actually, but you should know how easy it is to get turned on with these nipple piercings." She held her hands over her boobs. She was right, I did know.

"Just put a sock on the door this weekend if you can't handle it anymore." I nudged her, and she finally sat up.

"What are you two looking at?" She looked from Brandon to Parker and so did I.

"If you need help this weekend, I'm willing." Brandon gave Staci what would normally be a panty-dropping smile, but she only rolled her eyes.

"You got your nipples pierced?" This question was pointed at me, and I wasn't sure what to do other than blush.

"Yes. Staci did it."

Staci put her hand in the air, and I high fived her.

"Fuck." Parker ran his hand through his hair, and Brandon laughed.

As Parker climbed out of the car, Brandon turned toward us with a giant smile on his face. "This is going to be one interesting weekend."

...

We weren't in our room for five minutes before Staci was yelling at me to get my ass off my bed and start getting ready.

Apparently there was a meet and greet in the hotel bar for all the tattoo artists and the people who work in their shop. I didn't want to go. All I wanted to do was bury myself in the soft white sheets, but Staci was persistent to put it nicely. She actually dragged my ass out of the bed by my feet and threatened to undress me if I didn't get in the shower.

When I got dressed in a pair of black trousers and a white top, Staci was horrified.

"This is a tattoo convention, not a nun convention." She shook her head.

"I was trying to dress professionally since I am representing the shop."

"No one wants a tattoo from someone who's scared to show a little skin. Weren't you a stripper in your past life?"

I rolled my eyes at her but pulled my shirt over my head. I dug deep into my suitcase and pulled out the dress that I hadn't planned on wearing. I packed it as my safety net. You know, in case I met the man of my dreams this weekend, and he wanted to take me on a date. Now if that happened, I'd have to go shopping.

So here I stood in a cherry red mini dress that flowed out at my hips and had a dangerously low neckline. Staci was dressed similarly in a black dress that was simple and showcased the whirl of colors that marked her skin.

Actually, that was what made me stand out the most. My lack of tattoos. I ran my hand over my ribs and remembered the day Parker gave me mine. I could remember the feel of his hands working on my skin. I memorized the small scowl he had when he was concentrating. But mostly, I remember the ink that he marked my body with. Every line perfect, every color bleeding into my skin like it was meant to be there.

Staci locked her arm in mine and pulled me through the room with her. The place was packed. There were loads of women. Some were the most gorgeous I had ever seen, and there were some that had clearly spent their years living life to the fullest. Then there were the men. Some were scary looking with large beards and even bigger beer bellies, and some, hell, some were making me thank Staci for not coming down here dressed like a hermit.

In pure Staci style, she took us straight to one of the hottest guys in the room. I tried to pull away from her as she made a beeline for him, but she didn't let go of me until she wrapped her arms around him.

"Hey, Stac." He was talking to her, but as he pulled her tighter against his chest, he was staring at me.

He was tall, covered in tattoos and had hair so short that I could barely tell the color. But it was easy to see the bright blue of his eyes and the mischief they held.

"Liv, this is Neil." Staci pulled away from him and wagged her eyebrows at me.

I attempted to tell her to cut it out without Neil seeing me.

"Neil, this is Liv."

"It's nice to meet you, Liv." He pulled my hand in his, and he stared into my eyes as his strong hand shook mine.

"You too."

He had a hint of smile on his lips, and I found myself wanting to lean in closer to him. But the thought of Parker popped in my head. It seemed to happen any time I had the slightest interest in anyone else.

I searched the room for him, but he was nowhere to be seen. I wasn't even sure if he would be here. I assumed he would since Staci said all the artists came, but she hadn't specifically said he would be here.

Neil leaned against the bar behind him, and his leg brushed mine.

"Would you like to sit down?" He pulled the bar stool out for me.

I climbed up on the stool, and he was so close that the smell of his cologne surrounded me. It was light, yet masculine, and although I loved the smell of it, I loved another smell more.

"So Liv, what do you do?"

"I'm the receptionist at Forbidden Ink." I shrugged my shoulders because it seemed unimpressive compared to most of the people here.

"Ah. So that's how you know Staci." He held a glass of dark liquor in his hand, and I watched as he pressed it to his lips. "You work with Parker then, huh?"

I took a deep breath. "Yeah. I work with him." I scanned the crowd again and this time I saw him. He was making his way over to us, and he looked like a fucking sin. His hair was perfectly styled out of his face, and it seemed to only accentuate his strong jaw. He wore a solid black t-shirt and jeans, and somehow the intricate tattoos that covered his skin made them seem anything but simple.

"Hey, Neil."

"Hey, man." Neil immediately stood and hugged Parker then Brandon.

"I see you've met my girl, Livy." Parker looked at me as he said the words, but I only rolled my eyes.

"I didn't realize she was your girl."

"That's because I'm not." I piped in making Brandon chuckle.

Neil smiled at me before looking back to Parker.

Parker dropped his smile and looked at Neil head on. "She may not be mine now, but she was once and that means she's off limits."

"Are you kidding me, Parker?" I stood from my stool ready to smack him in the back of the head, but Brandon got to me before I could.

"Let's go dance, firecracker," he whispered in my ear while I stared daggers at Parker.

"I don't want to dance."

"Go dance, Liv. Have fun." Neil smiled at me before darting his eyes back to Parker. For what I wasn't sure? Approval.

"What a pussy," I said to myself causing Brandon to laugh as he pulled me away from the both of them.

There was a slow song playing and no one dancing in the large bar, but Brandon didn't care. He pulled me against him as if we were two people too in love to care what others thought about us.

"Why were you over there all snuggled up to Neil when you clearly still have feelings for Parker?"

"I do not have feelings for Parker. Why are you being such a cock block?" He twirled me around causing my dress to float around me before pulling me back against him.

"A cock block? If Neil got his cock anywhere near you, Parker would kill him."

"Parker's getting married. He doesn't have the right to care."

Brandon dipped me back, and the whole bar went upside down. When he lifted me back against his chest, I couldn't help but smile.

"Just because he's getting married doesn't mean it doesn't bother him."

I tried to pull out of Brandon's hold, but he held me firmly against him.

"So, he gets to parade his fiancée around like it doesn't fucking break my heart every time I see them together, but I can't talk to a guy because it might bother him." I blew out a frustrated breath.

"You're right."

"I am?" I asked confused.

"Yeah. You clearly don't have feelings for Parker anymore."

I buried my face in his chest, and he pulled me closer to him. "If it helps at all, I think he still has feelings for you as well."

"It doesn't," I murmured against his shirt.

"I didn't think so."

CHAPTER 18

A CRUEL DAMN JOKE

LIV

FOUR YEARS AND FIVE MONTHS EARLIER

"WHAT'S WRONG WITH YOU?" My brother was looking at me suspiciously, and I was worried that he knew about us.

"What are you talking about? Nothing's wrong with me."

"You're," he pointed up at my face, "all smiley and shit."

"I'm just happy, that's all." I shrugged my shoulders.

"Uh huh."

I could have told him the truth. I could have told him that I had just had the best night of my life with his best friend, but I wasn't that stupid.

"Is it because graduation is tomorrow? Nothing really changes except you don't have to go to school." He leaned his head against the back of the couch and changed the channel on the TV.

I hadn't even thought about graduation until he just mentioned it. I had been so distracted by Parker that I really hadn't thought about much else. I hadn't even decided where I was going to go to school. I had received a scholarship to the University of Tennessee and another to the University of Georgia.

But Parker made my decision easy. There was no way that I was going to leave him to go to Georgia. There was nothing that could make me make that decision.

"Yeah. I guess it is." I thought about the cap and gown that hung in my closet. Mason and Parker would be there to watch me walk across the stage in it. I'm sure my mother would be there somewhere as well if she remembered, but she would probably be late and she would probably be on the arm of some man I didn't recognize.

I spent the rest of the day getting everything ready for tomorrow. I ironed the soft pink dress that I would wear under my gown, and I laid out my shoes. I pulled out the one piece of jewelry I actually cared about, a simple string of white pearls that belonged to my grandmother. I didn't really know her well since my mother never took us to visit her, but she left the pearls to me in her will, and somehow, they felt special.

When I looked down at my outfit all laid out, I could feel the excitement bubble inside of me. Even though I wouldn't be leaving this place, I felt a piece of freedom settle into me that I had never felt before. I didn't know if it was graduation or Parker.

I lay on the floor and stared up at my ceiling. I had text Parker over an hour ago with no response. I felt a little needy, but I couldn't stand it. I picked up my cell phone and dialed his number.

As more rings passed, the more anxious I felt. Parker always answered my text or calls. Typically, he was the one reaching out first. I didn't know why but something about him not answering caused a knot to form in my stomach.

I thought about going to his house, but then I talked myself out of it. I didn't want to seem like a desperate, needy girlfriend. But was I even his girlfriend?

We hadn't even told my brother. I had no idea how we

would tell him because I was pretty positive on what his reaction would be. But I didn't care.

Parker was mine whether anyone else liked it or not.

I stood from the floor and tightened my ponytail. I needed to see him. It felt crazy not to see or talk to him after everything we shared last night.

When I pulled up to his house, I shook my head in disbelief. Madison's car was parked in his driveway. I trusted Parker, I really did, but that nagging feeling from before pulled tighter.

I parked my car behind Madison's and made my way to the front door. As I raised my hand to knock on the door, I saw him. Sitting across from her. Staring at her. She stood from the couch and moved next to him. Her leg touching his. Her hand reaching out for his much bigger one. When their hands connected and she laid them against her stomach, I felt like I couldn't breathe. All the air was sucked out of me along with every piece of happiness he had given me over the last few weeks.

I pressed my back against the door to hold myself up. *What was he doing? Why was she here?*

Tears formed in my eyes, but I prayed that I could keep it together at least until I got to my car.

I didn't know how long I stood there trying to get myself together. But when the door opened behind my back, I completely lost any composure that I had managed to gain.

The door closed quickly after it opened. I took a deep breath and looked up at Madison who was standing in front of me with her arms crossed.

"What are you doing here, Olivia?" Her voice was snarky and matched her face.

"I should be asking you the same." I stood from the step, refusing to look up to her.

"Olivia, I like you. I really do."

I rolled my eyes, and she continued.

"I don't want to see you get hurt."

"Then why are you with my boyfriend?" I pointed toward the house, and I could see the pity in her eyes.

"Boyfriend? That's funny. He didn't mention that and trust me, we've talked a lot while the two of you were doing whatever it is that you've been doing."

"I don't trust you, Madison." I pushed past her. No idea where I was going.

"Then would you like to feel?" I turned my eyes back to her and stared at her hands wrapped around her flat stomach. "It hasn't been kicking yet, but I can still feel our baby in there."

I jolted backward as if I had been kicked. I couldn't wrap my brain around what she was saying. I couldn't believe her.

I looked from her to the window, praying that Parker would come outside and tell me this wasn't true, but the door never opened.

"I'm still early," Madison continued to talk. "Only a couple of weeks."

My eyes flew back to hers, and I mentally did the calculations. She had to be further along than that because he had been with me. She covered her mouth with her hand and inhaled sharply. "Oh shit. You didn't know that we were still sleeping together while you all were hanging out."

I wanted to put my fist through her face, but I couldn't punch a pregnant girl no matter how badly I wanted to.

I didn't say another word to her. I didn't knock on Parker's door and demand that he explain himself. Instead, I ran. I ran straight to my car and flew out of his driveway all while Madison watched me. The tears poured from my eyes and clouded my vision as I made my way down the street.

My phone rang from the seat beside me and when I saw

Parker's name light up the screen, I cried harder. I didn't answer. I couldn't talk to him.

Instead, I went home, buried myself in my blankets, and prayed that this day was nothing more than a cruel damn joke.

CHAPTER 19

SLEEPING IS OVERRATED

PARKER

PRESENT

SHE WAS DRIVING me fucking crazy. When I saw her standing there with Neil, I thought I was going to lose my shit on him. Neil was a good guy. I had known him for a few years, and we had actually become pretty good friends.

The thought of Livy talking to him, laughing at the stupid shit he was saying, it made me feel like I was coming out of my skin.

I watched her dance on the empty dance floor with my best friend, and when I saw him turn the scowl that I had put on her face into a smile, I felt insanely jealous.

It wasn't right, I knew that, but it didn't change anything.

I spent the night tossing and turning in my bed while Brandon snored in his. It wasn't thoughts of my fiancée that was constantly clouding my vision and making it impossible to have a clear thought. It was a girl that I should have forgotten about years ago.

I tried to focus my thoughts on Emily, but no matter how hard I tried, I kept coming back to Livy. It was always fucking Livy.

I got up out of bed and pulled on a pair of sweats. If I couldn't sleep, I could at least go work out some of my built-up aggression. I made my way to the gym, passing by the indoor pool, and I caught a glimpse of her swimming laps.

I quietly made my way through the door; the only sound in the room was the splash of water as she glided through it. I took a seat in one of the pool chairs, and I watched her.

She finally came up for air, pushing her wet hair out of her face, and I watched as the rivets of water made their way down her body.

"Couldn't sleep?"

She jumped at the sound of my voice. Her hand flying to her chest. "You scared the shit out of me."

"Sorry." I chuckled. "I didn't mean to scare you."

She twirled her long hair in her hand, wringing out the pool water. "What are you doing down here?"

"The same as you, I suppose. Couldn't sleep."

She nodded her head in understanding and ran her hand through the water causing ripples in the otherwise calm pool.

"I'm sorry about earlier."

She looked up at me in surprise.

"I shouldn't have been a dick about you and Neil."

She searched my face, looking to see if I was being honest I suppose.

"You were being a dick."

"I know." I ran my hand through my hair.

"Why?"

"Isn't it obvious?" Our voices were barely a whisper, out of fear that we'd wake our memories.

"I don't get you, Parker." She climbed out of the pool and sat down next to me. "What do you want from me?"

"I don't know." I traced a drop of water with my finger until it disappeared at the crook of her elbow.

Her breathing was rushed, the loud inhale and exhale echoing off the walls and matching mine.

"I just..." She hesitated. "I... Goodnight, Parker."

She stood from her chair and again she hesitated like she had something more to say, but instead, she wrapped her towel tightly around her and left the room.

CHAPTER 20

CONGRATULATIONS

PARKER

FOUR YEARS AND FIVE MONTHS EARLIER

I HAD CALLED her phone six different times, and she didn't answer. Not once. My insides were in knots after talking to Madison, but not talking to Livy was worse. I felt like I was falling apart.

It was her graduation day so I knew she was probably busy getting ready for her big day, but I still felt like something was wrong.

Hell, everything was wrong.

I had tossed and turned in bed all night. I thought about what I should do. How I would tell my mom. How I would tell Livy. How the hell I was supposed to take care of a baby.

I wanted to ask Mason what she had been up to all day, but I knew he would be suspicious of my sudden interest in his sister. Instead, I sat quietly in the seat beside him as we waited for them to call her name.

After boring speech after boring speech, they finally called her name, Olivia Mae Conner. Mason and I jumped to our feet and screamed for her. Most of the graduates got a few cheers and claps, but not our Livy. We yelled as she walked across the stage looking gorgeous, but she didn't smile. When Mason blew his air horn that I was sure would get us kicked out, she didn't even laugh.

We sat down as she descended the stairs, and I didn't take my eyes off her. Some guy I didn't recognize put his hand up in a high five as they took their seats again, and she slapped it with a fake smile on her face.

I watched her the entire graduation, the entire ninety minutes, but she never looked my way. When it was time for them to throw their caps, she didn't throw it high in the air with no worry about where it would land, she just tossed it up, catching it a second later.

When she finally made her way to us after the ceremony, she instantly walked into her brother's arms. She didn't look at me. She just buried her face in his neck. When he finally let her go, I pulled her into me, not giving her a choice.

"Congratulations, Livy."

"Thanks," she said stiffly, her body just as stiff.

"What's wrong?" I whispered into her ear, but she didn't answer me. She just pushed out of my hold and faced her brother again.

"You're going to help me pack tonight, right?"

"For sure." Mason nodded his head.

"Pack for what?" I was starting to panic. What was she doing? Why wouldn't she talk to me?

"Our little Livy here got accepted to The University of Georgia on a full scholarship. She's been talking to her advisor, and she's decided to get an early start with summer classes."

"You're leaving." It was the only thing I could say, but there were a million thoughts running through my head.

I knew it was probably the best thing for her. As badly as I never wanted her to leave, I knew I would be toxic for her if she stayed.

"Yeah." She nodded her head. "I made the final decision last night. I move into my dorm this week."

All the air in the room seemed to disappear as she spoke. She didn't seem happy about her decision, she seemed determined. Determined to leave maybe. To get away from me.

"Congratulations, I guess." I felt more lost in that moment than I did when Madison told me I was going to be a father. I could handle a baby, I knew I could, but I wasn't sure if I could handle anything without Livy in my life.

"Congratulations to you too." She smiled, a fake smile that I fucking hated. "Madison told me the news."

I jolted back as if I had been hit. Madison told her? That bitch. I had been home all night worried about how I would tell Livy, and Madison just went and told her. The look on Livy's face was pure hatred, and although I thought she would be upset, I never expected that sort of reaction from her.

"What news?" Mason asked, completely forgotten.

"Oh, you didn't hear." Livy looked at her brother. "Parker is going to be a father."

CHAPTER 21

SWOON

LIV

PRESENT

I NEVER EXPECTED SO many people to be at this convention. The place was busting with people, and our booth seemed to be one of the most popular. Everyone was eager to meet Parker, Brandon, and Staci, but especially Parker.

People lined up and waited for hours for a chance to shake his hand and talk about a tattoo idea that they'd love for him to do. We had his portfolios laid out on the table of tattoos he had completed and drawings that were waiting for that perfect person.

Several people stopped on the photograph of my tattoo. After Parker made me lift my shirt up about ten times to show it off, Staci tied my white t-shirt up under my breast so it was on full display.

It made me feel a little uncomfortable considering the number of gawking men there were at the convention. Parker seemed uncomfortable with their staring as well, but more than that, he seemed proud to show off the work he had done on my skin.

We spent roughly eight hours at the convention, me passing

out business cards and scheduling appointments. By the time we made it to dinner, we were all dead on our feet.

"I'd say that was a successful convention," Brandon said as he cut into his steak.

"For sure." I nodded. "We booked almost fifty appointments."

"You did good today, Livy. Especially for your first convention," Parker was smiling at me, a genuine smile that I hadn't seen in a while.

A smile that made me feel things that I had no business feeling. It made me feel things that were too good to resist. It made me want to forgive him.

I wasn't mad at him because he got Madison pregnant. I could have lived with that. I would have supported him. But knowing that he cheated on me while I was falling so deeply in love with him killed me. It completely gutted me.

We finished dinner and made our way back to the bar. The place was packed again but we found a booth in the very far corner and the four of us piled in. Shots were poured and thrown back, and before long, I found myself giggling at everything Brandon had to say.

"Now that you have your first tattoo maybe Parker will loosen the reins a bit and let me ink some of that skin." Brandon winked at Parker, and Parker just rolled his eyes.

"I don't know, Brandon." I held my hand over my mouth to hide my chuckle. "Did you see the piece of art Parker put on me? I'm not sure if you can compare."

"Ouch." Brandon shook out his hand as if he had been burned, and Parker held up his hand to high five me.

We slapped hands, and Staci pulled Brandon's head onto her shoulder to comfort him.

"It's okay, Brandon. She's just saying that because she thinks Parker's hotter than you."

Brandon pulled his head off her shoulder and looked at me in shock. "You think he's more talented and hotter than me?"

"I didn't say that." I held up my hands in surrender.

"But is it true? Who do you think is hotter, me or Parker?"

Parker scoffed as if the question was preposterous, but I was tipsy enough that I didn't care.

"That's not a fair question, Brandon."

"Why not?" He crossed his arms.

"One," I held up my finger for emphasis, "he has those eyes." I motioned toward Parker's face. "Two, he has that bad boy thing going for him that girls can't seem to resist."

"What?" Brandon asked, irritated. "I'm just as much as a bad boy. I've got more tattoos than he does, and I can drink him under the table."

I waved my hand at him to stop his tirade. "Three." I cupped my hands around my mouth as I mock whispered, "I've seen his penis and let me just tell you." I wagged my eyebrows at him, and Staci fell over in the booth from laughing so hard.

"Okay." Parker chuckled. "I think that's enough."

"Says the hot one." Brandon pouted.

"Plus, he's all brooding and caveman like, and although it pisses me off ninety percent of the time, it also makes me swoon." I sighed dramatically then joined Staci in her infectious laughter, but Parker wasn't laughing with us.

He was watching me, too close, and I knew that I wasn't going to like what he had to say.

"I'm taking Livy to her room." He scooted out of the booth then stuck his hand out to me.

"I'm not leaving. I'm having fun." I winked at Staci as she continued to laugh.

"Livy, get your ass up before I carry you out of here."

"Swoon," Staci yelled out causing us both to erupt in another fit of giggles.

I bent over clutching my side from laughing so hard but then the entire room flipped on its head and my hip landed on Parker's shoulder.

"Parker!" I screamed. "Put me down."

He didn't answer me. He just kept walking with me bouncing against his shoulder.

I heard the ding of the elevator before the doors closed around us and Parker set me on my feet. I pushed my hair off my face and straightened my shirt that had bunched around my ribs.

"What's your problem? I was having fun." I leaned my back against the wall of the elevator because I was feeling a little lightheaded.

"Too much fun."

I waved him off. "No such thing. I was actually looking to have a little more fun tonight if you know what I mean."

I winked at him and his green eyes were on fire. I actually had absolutely no interest in sleeping with someone, but for some reason on that very night, I had all the interest in the world to get under Parker's skin.

"Don't say shit like that to me." His voice was so controlled, but it was easy to hear the anger that rested under the surface. It caused chill bumps to break out across my skin, and even though I knew I shouldn't, it made me want to push him further.

"Why not, Parker. We're friends, right?"

He just stared at me so I continued.

"It's been far too long since I've been laid. At least, not properly. You can tell me about you and Emily if you want to. Is the sex hot between you all? It was definitely hot between us once upon a time."

The doors opened in that moment, and I walked out with Parker on my tail. I stopped before getting to my room, and he ran into my back. I turned to face him, drunk on the alcohol and drunk on his proximity.

"Do you remember how you used whisper how desperate you were for me into my ear or is that something that you do with everyone?"

"It's not with everyone." He reached out for me, but I stepped out of his reach. He looked so vulnerable in that moment, but I wouldn't let it get to me. I learned a long time ago that I had to protect my heart when it came to Parker James.

"I don't believe you." I could barely hear my own words over my heart beat.

This time he didn't reach out for me. He slammed his body into mine, pressing my back against the wall, and his hands wrapped in my hair holding my face in place. "It was always you." He searched my eyes. "Always."

I shook my head trying to block out his words, but it was no use. They echoed through me making me doubt my decisions with every fading sound.

He growled in frustration.

"Listen to me." I continued to shake my head, but this time he didn't take no for an answer.

His hands tightened in my hair, and in the next moment, his lips pressed harshly against mine. I took a deep, shocked breath, and he took advantage of the moment, tasting my tongue with his.

My heart was pumping in my chest, my skin was covered in goosebumps, and I wasn't quite sure how to feel. What I did know was that I never wanted it to stop. I never wanted to be without his hands on me again.

His teeth clashed against my lip, dragging my bottom lip through his teeth, and I chased that taste of pain with my tongue.

I ran my hands over his chest, lifting his shirt to expose his tattooed skin, and he let me, throwing it behind him, not caring who found us like this in the hallway.

We were rushed, begging to get a taste of each other if only for a moment, and I cried out as his teeth ran across my neck.

I placed a kiss on his chest and my eyes caught the tattoo over his heart. A simple tattoo. A black date and nothing else.

"What is this?" I ran my fingernail over the ink as he ran his lips over the spot he had just bit.

He pulled away from me looking down and watching my fingers trace over his skin.

"That's the day you left."

We stared into each other's eyes, our breaths heavy along with our guilt.

"What now?" he asked the question that was screaming in my head. His face was so close to mine, and I could feel his breath against my lips. I brought my fingers to my mouth and tried to memorize the feel of his lips against mine.

I could still taste the adrenaline that pumped through my veins from the first day we kissed. I remembered how it felt to have his fingers dig into my skin as he pulled me closer to him, and I couldn't forget the desperation that I had for him then because I felt that desperation tenfold in that moment.

But then I remembered what it was like to have him destroy me, and no matter how easy it was to remember that high, it was impossible to forget that low.

I could see the panic in his eyes. The panic over who to choose. The indecision over what he really wanted, and I knew that I couldn't do this again. I could say that I was thinking about Emily, but I wasn't. I couldn't do this again because I feared he wouldn't choose me.

"How does it feel?"

"How does what feel?" He was searching my eyes looking

for something, and I prayed that whatever he was looking for he wouldn't find there. I prayed that I was strong enough to hide it.

"How does it feel to know that you're about to ruin someone else?"

I started to walk away from him, but he grabbed my hand, stopping me.

"Livy, don't."

"Don't what, Parker? You're about to get married. Go call your fiancée and don't worry about me. I'm sure you remember that I'm very good at keeping our secrets."

CHAPTER 22

FUCK FORGIVENESS

LIV

FOUR YEARS EALIER

TO SAY I was struggling would be an understatement. I was failing. As in my classes, college life, my life, I was failing all of it.

My roommate was the spawn of Satan. I guess that might be a little harsh, but when you share a space that could barely be considered a broom closet with a girl who gets angry if you even touch one of her pencils, it gets a little rough.

She didn't talk to me, and I didn't talk to her. Actually, I didn't really talk to anyone.

When I finally got to Georgia, faking my brave face in front of my brother became harder and harder. By the time he left me completely unpacked and organized in my tiny dorm, all I could do was lie in my twin size bed and cry.

I actually spent the first few days doing nothing other than that.

Chloe, my roommate, did ask me if I was dying on day three, but I was sure that was because she didn't want a dead body in her room, not because she gave a shit.

After that, I got up and tried my hardest to concentrate on

my classes, but every time I saw a couple laughing together or kissing, I had this irrational urge to go up to them and punch them both. It made me think about Parker and Madison.

Was he happy with her? Did he whisper into her ear while he made love to her? Did he ever think about me?

As soon as the thoughts ran through my head, the anger and the sadness would swarm me, and even attempting to pay attention to my professors was a lost cause.

I wasn't sure what I had done wrong. In actuality, I wasn't sure what the hell happened at all. I was Parker's best friend's little sister. He didn't seem that stupid, but it appeared that I didn't know him nearly as well as I thought.

There were moments when I considered running home and demanding that he tell me why. Demanding that he look me in the face and tell me that everything that happened between us was a lie, but the overwhelming fear that he would, crippled me.

I had been in Georgia for two months when my brother called me to tell me the news. I felt devastated for Parker, but I would be lying if I said I didn't feel some sort of relief. When Mason said the words miscarriage, my first thought was to run to him.

It didn't matter that he had hurt me. He was hurt, and I needed to get to him. I needed to do something.

But as soon as I had my keys in my hand, I remembered that he didn't want me. He had her.

"How is he?" I asked Mason.

"He seems okay. I mean he's upset, but he's also relieved. You know?"

"Yeah." I sat down on my bed and ran my hand over my comforter.

"I'm just glad he's not stuck with Madison forever. That

girl would have sucked the life out of him." My brother chuckled.

"Well that's who he chose." He chose her over me. I wanted to tell my brother that, but I couldn't.

"Not anymore," he laughed. "He's out on a date with some blonde we met last night."

I sucked in a deep breath. "He's already dating someone else?" The noose that seemed to be constantly around my heart pulled tighter.

"I wouldn't exactly call it dating. You know what they say about the best way to get over one girl is to get under another."

My brother didn't have a clue how his words would affect me, but as I closed my eyes, all I could see was him with someone else. I imagined how he would touch her. I imagined all the shit he was making her believe.

And in that moment, I knew that I would never forgive Parker James.

CHAPTER 23

CLUSTER FUCK

PARKER

PRESENT

I DIDN'T KNOW what I was thinking.

I was getting married.

Last weekend was, I couldn't say it was a mistake because nothing with Livy was ever a mistake, but it was a complete and utter cluster fuck.

After Livy disappeared into her hotel room that night, she kept her distance from me. She was friendly, in a way that made me feel like she felt sorry for me, but she was guarded.

She barely spoke to me all week at work. She nodded her head at me when I walked in the room, and she was fake friendly to me in front of my clients.

I needed a moment alone with her. I needed to talk to her. To see what was going on in that head of hers, but Emily made sure that I had absolutely no free time on my hands. We were having a pre-wedding celebration at the shop, whatever the fuck that meant, and Emily was in true bridezilla mode.

I had never seen anyone get so upset over appetizers or decorations, and with every word that came out of her mouth, I felt myself moving further away from her inch by inch.

By the time the party finally arrived, I was stressed out, confused as fuck, and in desperate need for a drink.

But even the whiskey couldn't wash down the taste of Livy.

Guilt flooded me whenever I was with Emily. I wanted to tell her the truth. I did, but selfishly, I was scared. What if I chose Livy, but she didn't choose me? I knew she was furious with me. It would take an idiot not to see that, but deep down, I knew that fire came from somewhere deeper than hate. What if she ran again? The last time she left, I was a complete fucking wreck.

I partied, I slept with more women than I should have, and every part of me ached with memories of her.

I couldn't be that guy again.

I refused to.

So instead of telling Emily that although I loved her, I was still insanely in love with Livy, I stood in my shop and sipped whiskey as if it would somehow be the answer to my problems.

Emily was in the corner talking to a group of her girlfriends, and as I watched them, I took in how vastly different we were. They were all a flourish of pastels and manners. My friends and I? We were on the complete other side of the spectrum. We looked as dark as the ink that marked our skin. Instead of glasses of champagne, I looked around at my friends and their hard liquor and beers.

Instead of the polite smiles that hid judgment of others, I watched Livy as she belly laughed at something Brandon was telling her. She didn't care who was watching. She didn't care how she looked, and there was something about it that made her the most beautiful thing in the room.

I made my way over to them subconsciously, but Livy quit laughing as soon as she spotted me.

"What's so funny?" I asked.

"Inside joke," Livy replied instantly, and I watched my best friend try to conceal his smile.

A tiny hand made its way across my chest and a moment later, Emily stood at my side. She lifted her chin to me, and I made the mistake of glancing at Livy right before my lips pressed against my fiancée's. She looked completely gutted, and it made me feel like the biggest piece of shit in the world to know that I was hurting her and Emily.

"So Emily..." Livy's face no longer had a trace of hurt on it. She was smiling as she looked at Emily. "Do you have any tattoos?"

"Oh, no." Emily chuckled.

"Why not?" Livy chuckled with her, a fake laugh that I fucking hated. "You're about to be married to one of the greatest tattoo artists on this side of the Mississippi. Surely, he isn't trying to charge you, is he?"

Emily smiled up at me, and I could see the pride in her eyes.

"No. He won't charge me. I'm just not sure that I ever want a tattoo."

That was news to me. Emily had never really shown an interest in my work, but I thought that eventually she would let me mark her with my art.

"Really?" Livy asked curiously. "I feel honored to have Parker's art on me."

She was fucking with my head. I wasn't sure if it was on purpose or not, but it didn't matter. She was making me question everything.

"Parker's tattooed you?" Emily actually seemed interested in the answer. More interested than she had ever been in my work before.

"Yeah." Livy nodded. "Hold this, Parker." She placed her

cranberry and vodka in my hand before she started pulling up her shirt to show her tattoo.

Emily tensed as the tattoo came into view and so did I. When Emily and I met, I was constantly drawing. Every free second of the day my hands were covered in pencil lead. I would constantly wake up in the middle of the night to draw, to clear my head, and there were too many occasions to count when Emily would wake up to me drawing.

To me drawing the tattoo that was now permanently a part of Livy.

Emily glanced up at me with accusation in her eyes before she looked back at Livy. "I love it."

"Me too. Could you imagine going through life without having something this beautiful from Parker on your skin?"

"No. You're right. I couldn't." Emily's hand squeezed around mine. "Parker, I think we should go mingle with the other guests."

"Oh, yeah. Sure." I handed Livy back her drink, and her eyes went from mine and Emily's clasped hands to look up at me.

"Have fun." She smiled, but I could see past it. I could see her falling apart in front of me, and I wanted nothing more than to reach out and catch her.

But Emily pulled on my hand in that moment, and Livy looked away.

CHAPTER 24

MINE

PARKER

FOUR YEARS EALIER

IT WAS two weeks after we found out about the miscarriage that I finally got the nerve to go to Georgia. I didn't really have a plan. I just knew that I wouldn't forgive myself if I didn't go. If I didn't talk to her.

I could have called her, and looking back, maybe I should have, but I needed to see her. I needed to see if she really cared as little about me as she was showing.

I knocked on her dorm room door and a girl with a don't-fuck-with-me face opened it.

"Can I help you?" She put her hand on her hip.

"Umm... yeah." I ran my hand through my hair. "I'm looking for Livy."

"Who?" She looked bored out of her mind.

"Livy?" When she still didn't look like she had a clue who I was talking about, I said, "Olivia?"

"Oh, you mean, Liv. She's not here." She started shutting the door, but I slammed my hand in the doorway just in time to stop her.

"Do you know when she'll be back?" I asked politely, my patience running thin.

"Probably in the morning. She went out with that guy again, and I told her that she wasn't bringing him back here so I assume she'll stay at his."

Her words crashed into me, forcing all the air out of my lungs. She was with someone else. She was... I could barely even think the words because they seemed so far gone now. She was mine.

"Do you want me to tell her that you stopped by?" Her roommate watched me as I completely fell apart in front of her.

I shook my head trying to form words. I had no right to feel this way. I had gone on a date with someone else after she left, but I went home after thirty minutes. It felt wrong. It wasn't her. I needed her.

"No." I finally found the words. "It doesn't matter anymore."

CHAPTER 25

911 TEXT

LIV

PRESENT

I STARED at myself in the mirror. I was wearing a pair of tight ripped jeans, a cute black top, and a pair of fuck-me heels. My hair was stick straight and my lips were cherry red.

I knew it was insanely stupid to say yes to a date offer when I really wasn't interested in the guy, but he was cute and I needed to get out of my own head. I met him at the coffee shop when I ran out to get coffee for everyone at the shop.

He was so nice and slightly charming, and even though I had been doing nothing but obsess over Parker, I decided to say yes.

When the doorbell rang, I tried to get there before my brother, but I'm pretty sure he had been pacing the living room waiting for him. I was twenty-two years old, but my brother still acted like I still needed a protector.

When I got to the door, Josh looked a little scared and a lot ready to get out of there. I pushed Mason into the house as I stepped out onto the front porch.

Josh didn't hug me in hello or let his eyes roam over my body. Instead, he watched the front door as he led me to his car.

As we walked into the restaurant, he seemed to finally breathe in relief.

"I'm sorry about my brother." I laughed. "He's a bit overprotective."

"Just a bit." He chuckled.

The server took our drink order, and Josh finally looked at me, his eyes jumping from my face to my chest.

"You look beautiful."

"Thank you." I smiled. It was a little late, but I kept that to myself.

"So Liv, what do you do?"

"I'm a receptionist at Forbidden Ink. Do you have any tattoos?"

I took a sip of my sweet tea and watched him shake his head.

"No way. I can't have any tattoos at my job."

"Why not?"

"I'm a lawyer. No one wants someone to represent them that looks like a convict themselves."

He laughed, but I didn't.

"You don't like tattoos?"

"No." He shook his head again with a smile on his face. "You don't have any do you?"

"I do."

He straightened up at that.

"Oh. I haven't seen one."

You probably never will either. "It's hidden."

"See that I can deal with. If you can put on clothes and still look presentable, I think they are fine."

I thought about what Parker would think about his words as they flowed from his lips, and if I were half as courageous as Parker, I probably would have said his thoughts out loud. But I wasn't.

I nodded my head as Josh continued to talk. I wasn't sure what Parker wanted from me anyways. He tracked my every movement with his eyes as I worked around the shop, but we still hadn't spoken a word about our kiss.

Our drunken, idiotic kiss.

He was getting married in two weeks. Two fucking weeks, and I was sitting on the sidelines obsessing over a kiss. He probably thought it was a mistake. He was probably just worried that I would say something to Emily, but I would never do that to him.

As much as we had hurt each other in the past, I wanted to see him happy. Even if that meant he was with someone else.

"Do you want children, Liv?"

"Whoa. That escalated quickly." I laughed, but Josh didn't. "Yeah. I want kids." I just wanted them to have striking green eyes and Parker's sense of humor.

"Me too. I think I want four."

I was thinking two, but I didn't say that to him. I just nodded my head.

Our food arrived at the table and I was thankful for the distraction.

We chatted as we ate. The topics were much less serious, and I finally started to relax.

Josh liked to hike which was something that I thought I might enjoy.

I told him how much I loved the lake, and he told me that he preferred the beach.

My phone vibrated in my lap, and I looked down at my text.

STACI: **How's the date going?**

. . .

IT'S GOING.

STACI: **Well that sounds tantalizing. We're going out for drinks later. Bow out of the date earlier and come with!**

OKAY. **Let me see what I can do.**

STACI: **911 text me if you need help!**

"IS EVERYTHING OKAY?" Josh asked as he handed the server his card.

"Yeah. Sorry. It's just my best friend."

"Is this a 911 text?" He chuckled and guilt filled me.

"No. She actually wanted to know if we wanted to meet her and some of my other friends out for a drink. Would you be interested?"

"Sure." He smiled, and I tried to make myself feel something. I knew it was

insane to think the curve of someone's lips could make you fall for them, but I had done it before. I stared at Josh's smile, the edges of his lips perfectly symmetrical, and I longed for something a little less perfect. I craved the small dimple on Parker's right cheek as his smile lifted higher on that side, and I felt anxious to feel his bottom lip that was just slightly fuller than the top one between my teeth.

But that smile didn't belong to me, and I needed to do myself a favor and remember that.

CHAPTER 26

THE OTHER GUY

PARKER

PRESENT

"WHERE'S LIVY?" Staci was talking to Mason, but my attention was focused solely on them as soon as I heard her name.

"She's on a date."

My heart stopped at his words.

"With who?" Staci seemed excited for her, and I wanted to ask her whose team she was on.

"Some guy she met at a coffee shop. I wasn't too impressed with him." Mason shrugged his shoulders.

I wanted to ask him where they went, but I didn't need him suspicious of me. Not to mention my fiancée who was sitting by my side glued to her cell phone.

Staci pulled out her cell phone as well and started texting before a smile lit up her face.

"She's going to come by here after." She looked directly at me as she said the words, and I narrowed my eyes at her. She and Livy had become best friends ever since Livy started working at the shop, and I wondered how much Livy had told her.

"Are you almost ready?" Emily wrapped her arm around mine.

"We just got here like thirty minutes ago, Emily," I whispered to her, and she just rolled her eyes before going back to her phone.

I knew that it was stupid, but I wanted to be here when Livy came. It was driving me insane to think about her on her date. Did she like him? Would it become something serious?

I downed a few beers as I watched the door waiting for her to arrive. My friends were all laughing around me, and I tried to join in, but every time the door opened I was on alert.

When she finally walked through the door, I finally breathed a sigh of relief. Until I saw some douchebag walk in behind her.

He was wearing a baby blue button-down shirt and black dress pants, and as much as I hated to say it, he actually looked like he fit next to her. Staci waved her hand in their direction, and Livy's face lit up when she saw her.

She made her way over to us, and she faltered slightly when she saw me. Apparently, Staci didn't tell her that I would be here.

Her date pulled out her seat for her directly across from me before sitting down himself. I gave him points for being a gentleman, but that didn't make me want to rip his head off any less.

"Hey, guys. This is Josh."

We all said our hellos, and Brandon shook his hand. Emily had finally put her phone down, and she was looking directly at Livy. I wasn't exactly sure what the look was about, but I could see a glimpse of the catty Emily that I didn't like.

"Hey, Emily." Liv smiled at her, and Emily smiled back.

I watched Josh as he put his arm over the back of Livy's chair, but she didn't seem to notice. I watched him watching her as she and Staci gabbed on about who only knows what. He looked like a good enough guy, but he wasn't good enough for her.

Livy would glance my way every so often, but as soon as I caught her gaze, it'd dart away.

I left the table to order a round of shots, and Brandon followed me.

"What are you doing?" he asked as I threw a shot of whiskey down my throat.

"Getting drunk," I said sarcastically.

He rolled his eyes. "That's not what I mean. What are you doing with Livy?"

"Livy's on a date." I looked behind me to watch her date lean in close to talk to her.

"And you're here with your fiancée yet you both continue to eye fuck each other regardless."

I ran my hands through my hair. "No. We're not."

"Yes. You are. Everyone can see it except maybe you, Livy, and Emily. Even her date's been watching her watch you. Now I'll ask you again, what the fuck are you doing?"

I threw another shot back and stared at my best friend. "What do you expect me to do?"

"Break up with Emily for starters."

"It's not that easy." I shook my head. I had been thinking about ending things with Emily ever since Livy came out from behind that curtain at the strip club, but I would crush her. "We're not just dating, Brandon. I'm supposed to marry that girl in two weeks." I looked over at Emily who was still sitting on her phone and ignoring all my friends that surrounded her. She looked so out of place with them, so out of place with me.

"And did you hear how thrilled you are about that? You just said that you're supposed to marry her. Not that you're going to, not that you can't wait, but that you're supposed to." He shook his head like I was the biggest idiot he had ever met. "You're not supposed to marry someone because you're scared of hurting them, Parker. You're supposed to marry someone who sets you on fire. Someone who you can't stop thinking about and who thinks about you more than they do themselves." He took a deep breath and stared me straight in the eye. My usual jokester friend completely serious in that moment. "I heard a quote once that if you want to know what someone loves then you should look at what they photograph. I think that goes for drawing too. How many portraits have you secretly drawn of Livy even since you and Emily have been together? How many drawings have you titled something else, but they only remind you of her?"

I stared at him and let his words sink into me.

"What about Mason?" I looked at my other best friend who now had his sister in a hug as they laughed.

"Fuck, Mason. If he can't see how much you love his sister, then he's as much an idiot as you are."

CHAPTER 27

SHE DOESN'T GET EVERYTHING

LIVY

PRESENT

I FELT like every day I was fighting a war with myself. Some days I would wake up and nothing in the world mattered as much as Parker. Other days, the pain was so fresh that the only thoughts that ran through my head were how to destroy him like he had done me.

I didn't know what I had expected after our kiss, but I didn't think that everything would be exactly like it was before. Parker barely seemed to notice me at work, and Emily was there far more than she had ever been before.

Their wedding was a week away, and I swear to God if I had to listen to her talk about it for one more minute, I was going to strangle her.

With every detail that she described, it was as if she was stabbing a tiny dagger into my heart. Part of me wondered if she was aware of what she was doing to me, but I couldn't be certain. She was too friendly, blissfully happy, and I hated her.

Parker was busy with a client, and I was still trying to figure out why the hell Emily was still here. We weren't friends, regardless of how hard we had tried, and I was beyond ready for her to leave.

"So... I took your advice."

"You did." I was staring at the computer adjusting Parker's schedule.

"Yeah. I'm finally going to get a tattoo."

I looked up at her, and she was clearly watching me.

"Have you decided what you're going to get?"

She nodded her head excitedly. "You have to promise not to tell, Parker though. It's going to be a wedding surprise."

"Okay."

She pulled out a wrinkled piece of sketch paper that had clearly seen better days, and as I stared down at the drawing, I thought I was going to hyperventilate.

"Where did you get this?" I held the drawing between my trembling fingers, and I tried to stop the bombarding memories from taking over.

"I found it in an old notebook of Parker's that he had hidden away. I absolutely love it. Don't you?"

I did love it, but not for the same reasons she did. If she knew why I loved it, she would hate it.

I laid the drawing on my desk, and I stared down at the portrait of a girl, a girl I hadn't known for a very long time. Half of her face peaceful and half her face distorted with a swirl of colors and lines.

It was the first drawing Parker had ever drawn of me, but I looked nothing like that girl anymore.

I searched the lines, looking for something, but no matter how hard I looked, all I could see was Parker and me. It was the perfect match to the tattoo that was inked over my ribs, and there was no way in hell I was going to let her get it.

"I love it." I croaked out the words. "When do you plan on surprising Parker? I can block some time out of his schedule."

"I'm thinking the week after the honeymoon. I would get it before the wedding, but I wouldn't want anything to ruin our wedding night if you know what I mean." She winked at me, and I could taste vomit rising in my throat.

I blocked time off in his schedule then put the drawing in a folder. "I'll keep it safe until the appointment so he doesn't find it."

"Thank you, Liv. I couldn't have done this without you."

"You're welcome."

"We're going to match, you know?" She smiled.

"What?"

"Me and Parker. You've probably never seen it before because the tattoo is over his ribs, but he has this same tattoo on him. I'm so damn excited."

I couldn't breathe as the words passed her lips. I wanted to tell her that I was the one who inspired the tattoo she wanted. I wanted to tell her that I refused to allow her to get this drawing, but instead, I smiled and watched her sashay out the front door.

I pulled the drawing back out of the folder and held it in my hands thinking about what I wanted to say to Parker. I considered hiding the drawing and claiming that I lost it, but I couldn't do that. Plus, he apparently had a perfect match permanently inked on his body.

When he finally appeared out of his room with his client, I held my breath trying to calm myself down. I knew I had no business getting this worked up, but it was impossible to tell your heart not to care when it had done nothing but care for so long.

As soon as his client walked out the door and Parker locked the door behind him, closing up for the night, I stormed over to him and lifted his shirt so I could inspect his body.

It only took a moment to spot my face, and I ran my hand over the ink as a tear trailed down my cheek.

"What the hell are you doing, Livy?" He tried to pull his shirt down, but I refused to let him.

"Why do you have this?" He opened his mouth to respond, but I spoke again before he could. "She's not fucking getting it, Parker. Over my dead body."

"What are you talking about?"

I stormed over to my desk, and he followed me. I shoved the drawing at him, and he stared down at it before looking back up at me.

"Where did you get this?"

"Your fiancée brought it in. She plans to surprise you by getting it after your honeymoon."

"Livy." He reached out for me, and I let him.

"I swear to God, Parker. She's not fucking getting it. She doesn't get everything. This is mine."

He pulled me into his chest, squishing the drawing between us. "I won't, Livy. I promise I won't tattoo it on her. But you have to tell me what you want. Do you want me to leave her for you? Do you want me to tell her that I still love you?"

"That's not fair." I stepped away from him.

"No. What's not fair is that you came back into my life when I finally thought that I had something real. You make me question everything, Livy. Everything."

"I didn't come back here to ruin your life, Parker. You know that. You were there, bringing me back here." I could taste salt on my lips, and the taste of my pain a fresh reminder of everything we've been through. "I just need to think."

I walked past him into the back room, but his steps echoed mine, following me step for step.

"You're not running again, Livy." He grabbed my hand, pulling me to a stop.

"We've been through too much." I shrugged my shoulders.

"But no matter what, I can't unlove you, Parker." I whispered the words as he tucked my hair behind my ear.

"I don't want you to."

He lifted me in the air as his mouth crashed into mine. My back slammed into the wall, and I tightened my thighs around him.

I didn't have time to think about whether what we were doing was right or wrong. I could only think about how badly I wanted him, and as he pulled my shirt over my head, I did absolutely nothing to stop him.

The door to his and Brandon's office crashed against the wall and my back hit the cold wood of his desk. I searched his eyes, but there wasn't an ounce of indecision there as he pulled my pants down my legs.

He didn't give me a chance to catch my breath let alone my conscious as he began nipping at the delicate skin of my thighs. I let my head fall back against his desk as his breath trailed over me. The moment his mouth pressed against my panties, I thought I was going to die. He ran his tongue over the fabric which was already wet with want, his hands wrapping around my thighs, and when he jerked me to the end of the desk, my body colliding with his, I cried out in pleasure.

He stared down at me, his eyes roaming over every inch of my skin, and his hand running over my tattoo. His hand trembled precariously close to my breastbone, and I watched him, the exact moment the last ounce of his control snapped visible before my eyes. His fingers curled into the edge of my panties and then the fabric was shredded as he ripped it from my body.

I couldn't catch my breath as he flipped me over the desk, my face pressed against the wood, my ass on full display.

He gripped my hips in his rough hands before he finally slammed into me. The desk scraped against the floor, too weak against his power, and I gripped the edge as he slid into me over and over.

I had never felt like this before, engulfed so completely by someone else. Every inch of my skin dying for his touch. He gripped his hand in my hair, standing me up before he sat down in his chair pulling me down on top of him.

I began moving my body against his as he wrapped his arms around my torso. I looked down at his inked skin, so beautiful, and I laced my trembling bare hand in his. He lifted our hands together, pressing them against my chin, turning my face toward his, and I got lost as his lips devoured mine.

I didn't think about how much we had hurt each other. I didn't think about his fiancée. Not a trace of our ghosts or an ounce of fear of our future lived in that space. It was only me and Parker, and as his fingers dug into my hips, I fell apart around me.

Spiraling out of control. I never wanted to stop, because for the first time in a very long time, I felt like I wasn't broken anymore. The madness inside me settled, and I knew, that no matter what happened from this moment forward, I would never recover from Parker James.

CHAPTER 28

KNIGHT IN SHINING FUCKING ARMOR

PARKER

PRESENT

I WAS SUCH A FUCKING FOOL. When Livy was in my arms, I felt like I was finally alive again. I breathed her in, filling my lungs, and I never wanted to know what it felt like to not be able to breathe again.

But when I woke up on the floor of my office twenty minutes before I was supposed to be at the wedding venue for our rehearsal, I woke up alone. I jumped from the floor, pulling my jeans on, and searching the space for a single trace of her. The contents of my desk were scattered on the floor and my skin was covered with the scent of her perfume. I looked around the room remembering the night before, and I pulled at my hair in frustration.

When I had fallen asleep, it was with her in my arms. We didn't speak of the future. We didn't make each other any promises, but that didn't matter to me. I thought... I fucking thought that last night meant something to both of us.

I grabbed my phone out of my pocket. Ten missed calls from Emily lit up my screen, but I quickly cleared them away. I would deal with Emily. I had to, but right now, Livy was the only thing on my mind.

I hit her name and the phone shook in my hand as I listened to each ring while holding my breath. When she didn't answer, I quickly called her again. This time, her voicemail picked up on the third ring and thought I was going to lose my fucking mind.

I threw my shirt over my head and headed to my car while dialing Brandon's number.

"Hey, man."

"Hey. Have you seen her?" My voice was rushed and heart felt like it was beating out of my chest.

"Yes. She's here at the church where you're supposed to be. Where are you?"

I stopped in my tracks. "She's at the church?"

"Yeah, man, and she's already bossing everyone around. You better get here before I kill her."

"Who are you talking about?"

"Your fiancée. Who the hell are *you* talking about?" He was whisper-yelling into the phone.

"Livy. I have to find her."

"It's about fucking time."

"Can you cover for me there?" I had no clue what I was going to do, but I knew I wasn't going to that church.

"Of course."

I drove to Livy's house and banged on the door like a maniac, but no one answered. Her brother would be at the church with my other friends, and irrationally I wanted to kill him for not being home so I could search for her.

I went to Staci's house next.

She opened the door wearing nothing but a long t-shirt, a messy bun on the top of her head, and a death stare.

"Stac, is she here?"

She put her hands on her hips. "You have a lot of nerve, Parker."

"I don't have time for this. Is she here?"

When she didn't answer me, I stormed past her and started looking around her apartment.

"Are you insane? What the hell do you think you're doing?" Staci was following me around her space, but I didn't care what she had to say. I wouldn't let Livy run again.

"You are her best friend, Staci. Where is she?" I sounded frantic, and I could see a trace of pity in her eyes before she looked away. "I can't let her run again. I can't handle it."

"Did you ever stop to think about why she ran?"

"We're both scared..."

Staci shook her head interrupting me. "No, Parker. You just cheated on your fiancée with her."

"So you've talked to her."

She held up her hand. "She ran the first time because you cheated on her and destroyed the girl that she was. She can't live with herself knowing that she's helping you do it to someone else."

"What?"

Staci opened her mouth to talk, but I interrupted her. "I never cheated on her."

"It's a little late for that, Parker. She knows that you were sleeping with that girl you got knocked up when you were with her." She rolled her eyes at me, and it was as if everything finally clicked into place.

Livy thought I cheated on her. That was why she ran. That was why she left me.

"I swear to God, Stac. I never cheated on her. I fucking love her. I always have."

Staci looked at me, watching me closely, trying to see if what I was saying was the truth. I bit my tongue as she took her time. I knew if I snapped at her again then she would never tell me where she was.

"Please," I begged.

"I can't tell you, Parker." She shook her head. "You're not ready."

"What the fuck do you mean I'm not ready? Trust me. I've been in love with that girl for over four years. I'm more than ready."

"What about Emily?" She hopped up onto her kitchen counter and pulled a spoon out of a tub of icing that sat in the fridge.

"I'll deal with Emily, but I have to get to Livy."

She shook her head like I was the biggest idiot in the world. "What you need to do is deal with Emily before you go anywhere near Livy. You can't go to her like this." She waved her spoon in my direction. "You look half-crazy in your after-sex glow. If you want to do this right, then you have to be in it one hundred percent. You can't be confessing your love to Livy when you still have a ring on another girl's finger. Take my advice on this. I read a lot of romance novels."

"Okay." I ran my hands through my hair. "Okay, but will you promise me that you won't let her run."

"I'll see what I can do." She plopped the spoon filled with icing in her mouth.

"I'm not kidding, Staci. I can't fucking live without her again. I won't."

"Then get on your white horse there buddy and figure out how to be her knight in shining fucking armor."

I kissed her on her forehead, her hair smelling of vanilla icing and making me question exactly how much she's had to eat.

"I owe you one." I started walking toward the door.

"Yeah, yeah. You can pay me in ink."

CHAPTER 29

GRAND GESTURE

LIVY

PRESENT

"HE'S GONE." Staci poked her head into her spare bedroom.

"I heard." I was sitting on the edge of her guest bed trying to take in everything that had happened.

"Did you hear what he said?" She plopped down on the bed next to me.

"Yes, but does it really change anything?" I fell back onto the bed and stared up at her ceiling.

"Well, I guess the real question is, do you believe him? If the answer is no, then no, it doesn't change a damn thing. If the answer is yes, then it changes everything."

I watched the ceiling fan spin around and around as I thought about her words. Did I believe him? Without a doubt, but I also didn't know if that was just me being foolish or not. I had believed every word that ever left his mouth once upon a time.

I had believed that nothing would ever come between us, but it did.

I thought about everything we had been through, all the shit that we had let keep us apart, and I knew that no matter what, after all this time, I wanted nothing more than to be with Parker James.

"I believe him."

Staci clapped her hands scaring the crap out of me. "So what's the plan?"

"The plan?" I turned my head to look at her.

"Oh, dear God. Do none of you know what romance is? We must have a plan. Some grand gesture to let him know that you still love him as much as he loves you."

"I don't have a plan." I groaned.

"I know." Staci bounced on the bed. "You can get your vagina pierced."

"What kind of romance are you reading?" I balked.

"True. Wrong genre." She jumped off the bed and pulled me with her into her bedroom.

"What are we doing?" I asked as I stared at her floor to ceiling bookshelves that were covered in books of every color.

"Research."

CHAPTER 30

FUCK YOU, PARKER

PARKER

PRESENT

TELLING EMILY only a few days before our wedding that I was in love with someone else was a huge mistake. I should have broken it off with her the moment Livy walked back into my life, but I was an idiot.

She was furious. Livid. But she didn't look heartbroken.

She threw a vase of flowers at my head the moment the words "I can't do this" left my lips.

"What do you mean, you can't do this?" She seethed.

"I'm not trying to hurt you, Emily. I swear, but you know as well as I do that we're not meant to be together."

"No. What I know is that we have over two hundred guests coming to our wedding in less than a week."

"I know. I'm sorry." I looked around the room at the wedding decorations that were waiting to be shown off on our big day.

"You're sorry. You're fucking sorry?" she yelled. It was one of the first times I had ever heard Emily cuss. "My dad was right about you, Parker. You're fucking trash."

I nodded my head and bit my tongue. I was breaking the girl's heart. I deserved every bit of hate she was throwing at me.

"I'm so fucking glad I never let you tattoo me. God, I couldn't imagine having that shit on me for the rest of my life."

I rubbed the back of my neck and took a deep breath. "Tell your dad that I'll cover all the cost of the wedding."

"We don't want your pity money, Parker. Just leave."

"Emily." I reached out for her. Regardless of what happened, I didn't want to hurt her. I never meant to hurt her.

"Don't fucking touch me." She stared at me, the girl I was prepared to marry, a girl who I loved, but she was looking straight through me. "You should know that I cheated on you at my bachelorette party." She crossed her arms over her chest.

I listened to her words, but they didn't hit me like they should have. They didn't affect me at all. "I'm sorry I hurt you, Emily. I'm truly sorry."

I started walking to the door, but her next words stopped me.

"You still love her, don't you?"

"What?" I turned to look at her.

"I'm not stupid, Parker. You don't draw a portrait of a girl who looks exactly like her for years for no reason."

We stared at each other for a long minute with neither of us saying anything.

"Yes. I'm still in love with her."

She toyed with the diamond ring on her hand before sliding if off her hand and placing it on the table in front of her. "Fuck you, Parker."

CHAPTER 31

REGRETS

LIVY

PRESENT

IT HAD BEEN a week since I had laid eyes on him. I took Staci's advice and read as many romance books as a girl could while she was hiding out, but I didn't feel a bit closer to having any idea what I was supposed to do.

I wanted to run to him. I did, but Staci had told me that he had been dealing with canceling the wedding and all the drama that went along with that and I knew he didn't need me complicating matters.

But he canceled his wedding.

His fucking wedding.

For me.

I searched the backs of her paperbacks for a story about high school sweethearts who had completely fucked up everything trying to love each other, but no matter how hard I looked, I couldn't find our story.

I read about a firefighter who stormed into a building braving the blazing fire to save the girl who was stranded on the fifth floor and how they lived happily ever after, and I almost threw the book through the wall.

Parker's and my love story wasn't a perfect romance novel. It was complicated, filled with lies, heartbreak, and secrets. I didn't know if we could ever get past everything we had been through.

If we were worth the fight.

Staci had been at work all day, and I had only moved off the couch to eat our leftover pizza from the night before. I was wearing an oversized t-shirt that I had stolen from Parker when I was eighteen years old, and I hadn't brushed my hair for as long as I could remember.

When there was a knock on the door, I considered not answering it. No one needed to see me like this, but no one knew I was here. But it was probably a package from Amazon since Staci ordered paperbacks about three times a week like a hoarder. I told her that there was no way she could fit any more on her shelves, but she looked at me like I had just given her the most welcome challenge.

I pulled the door open, squinting as the sunlight flooded her living room, and then I stared at Parker.

He looked so damn handsome. He always had, but he also looked tired. Dark circles shadowed his normally bright eyes.

I stepped out of the doorway to let him in, and I fidgeted with the edge of my t-shirt as we stood in awkward silence.

"I'm sorry." His voice was rough, and I could feel the rumble of it throughout my whole body.

"I know."

"No. You don't." He stepped toward me. His body only a few inches away from mine. "I'm sorry that I didn't tell your brother how I felt about you when I was sixteen years old. I'm sorry I made you feel like I didn't love you even though you ran through my every thought every single day."

I shook my head to stop him, but he continued.

"I'm sorry that I dated Madison when I imagined she was

you every time we touched. I'm sorry that I let her come between us when it should have been me and you against the world. I'm sorry that I let you leave. I'm sorry that I didn't demand you come back with me when I showed up at your dorm and you were on a date with someone else."

"What?" I asked, but he held up his hand.

"I need to get this out. Okay?"

I nodded my head.

"I'm sorry that I ever tried to forget you. I'm sorry that I tried to love Emily while I secretly drew your face in my sketchbook every night. I'm sorry..." He swallowed, and I watched his throat work. "I'm sorry that I made love to you when I wasn't one hundred percent yours. If I could go back, I would change it all."

Tears were running down my cheeks, and he reached up and caught them with his thumbs.

"But my biggest regret, something I will live with for the rest of my life, is that you didn't know how much I have loved you since I was sixteen years old. Every day, every single day, I have loved you. As much as I tried," he cupped my chin in his hand. "I have never figured out how to not be madly in love with everything you do."

I couldn't stop the tears from flowing down my cheeks, and as I tried to catch my breath, I hiccupped, causing Parker to laugh.

He pressed his lips against mine softly, just the faintest touch, and I felt everything inside me settle. He lifted me in the air, my legs instantly wrapping around him, and he set me on top of the kitchen counter.

"But my grand gesture?"

"What?" Parker looked at me like I was crazy as he ripped his old t-shirt over my head.

"Staci told me I had to do a grand gesture. Like that book I just read. He saved her from a fire, and they fell in love. I was supposed to save you from a fire or something. I should have bought a fireman's outfit."

Parker lowered his face to look at me, staring at me for a long moment before he said, "Babe, trust me when I tell you, you have saved me."

His movements were hungry but reserved. I could practically feel his tension radiating under my fingertips. He was so controlled and so restrained.

I hated it.

I didn't want him to love me tenderly. I wanted him to bury his hands in my hair and get lost in me. I wanted him to bruise my lips and stain my skin with his need. I wanted him to dig his fingers into my soul and make love to the storm inside me. I wanted him to remind me how to breathe by taking my breath away, to love me recklessly. I didn't need his hesitant touch or guarded desire. What I needed was to feel his fire and know that I wasn't burning alone.

He drug his bottom lip against mine. Not a kiss. A barely there touch. But I still felt my body arching off the counter, begging for more. My tongue tracing the shape of his lips.

"Please, Parker." I pulled his shirt over his head and threw it behind me.

His hands in my hair tightened and his gentle lips became demanding. No longer was there a calm tease of tongues or slow drag of lips. His mouth was punishing against mine. Teeth clashed, tongues dueled, and hearts pounded against one another.

My hands dug into his back holding him close to me and his hips settled between my open thighs. I barely had any clothes on, but I felt like I was on fire. My skin burned under his touch.

He pulled away from my mouth and trailed kisses down my neck. His hands worked their way down my body before jerking my hips closer to him. I could feel his hardness pressed against me, and I was dying to remove all the barriers between us.

My fingers fumbled with the button of his jeans, and I had to slow my trembling hands down to accomplish the task. He stepped back away from me before helping me to my feet. With a flick of his fingers, my bra fell to the floor and he stared at my breasts, his eyes becoming feral.

Before I even realized it was happening, his hands gripped my ass, he lifted me in the air, and he slammed me back on top of the counter. The cool granite hit the overheated skin of my back, and I arched away, the sensation too much. Parker took that as an opportunity to drag my nipple into his mouth. His tongue flicking rapidly, his teeth causing a delicious ache.

The strands of his hair were gripped tight in my fingers, and I didn't know where I wanted him more. I needed him everywhere. My body craved the touch of his hands. It begged for the trace of his lips.

His mouth worked its way down my body hearing my silent request, and I squirmed on the counter as he traced the curve of my hips with his tongue. His fingers hooked into the side of my black panties, and he slowly dragged them down my trembling thighs. His mouth never leaving my skin.

He nipped at the sensitive skin of my thighs. His tongue, lips, and teeth teasing me and drawing out my short, rapid breaths. He looked up at me then. His eyes staring straight into mine while I silently begged him to put me out of my misery.

"I've missed you so damn much, Livy."

I wanted to tell him that I had missed him too. He needed to know how much I loved him, but he didn't give me a chance. Instead, he took away my voice and my breath with a swipe of his tongue. The only sound I could manage was screaming out his name.

I didn't think about the fact that we were in the middle of my best friend's kitchen. I wouldn't have cared if she busted in the door. There was only one thing on my mind and that was falling apart with Parker in that moment. Nothing else mattered.

He watched me as he devoured my flesh. It was both erotic and tense, and I loved every minute of it. The power he possessed over me in that moment fueled me.

My orgasm built quickly. My trembling legs tightened around Parker's head and my hands in his hair clenched to fists. I was right on the edge just waiting for that final push.

But instead of falling over the brink, I shot my head up when Parker's mouth left my body and I no longer felt his warmth. He didn't leave me alone for long. He slammed into me with a power that caused my body to slide across the counter, but his hand was there to easily pull me back to him.

His tongue dipped between my breasts tasting the sweat that trickled there before he worked his way to my earlobe.

"You need to hold on, Livy," he whispered softly into my ear. "Because you have no fucking idea how bad I want you."

He pulled my leg around his waist, his fingers dug into my hips, and then he kept his promise and gave me a reason to hold on.

He thrust into me repeatedly pushing me further into euphoria. My body clenched around him. My heart clenched in my chest.

It didn't slip my mind that I hadn't said it out loud yet, but when I looked up and saw those bright green eyes staring down at me, our bodies intertwined, and our hearts beating against one another in our chests, I knew that he knew I was in love with him. I felt like it was radiating from me. Pouring out of every pore.

He lifted me from our position and turned me so my chest

was now pressed against the cold granite. He slid into me and my back slid against his chest. He moved my hair off my shoulder and tasted the sensitive skin of my neck. He felt so incredibly close to me even though I couldn't see him. But God, I could feel him.

"Look how goddamn beautiful you are." His hand gripped my jaw and turned my face to look at the mirror that hung over Staci's dining room table.

I could see myself in the reflection. My body completely controlled by Parker. His hands were roaming over my body leaving a trail of chill bumps in their wake. I could see his face watching us in the mirror, and I didn't want to hide. I wanted him to see all of me. I wanted to be laid completely bare.

I looked at us in the mirror, his skin covered in tattoos, a fucking piece of art, and when I looked down at the heart he had created so perfectly inked on my body, I knew that all the madness in my heart was meant for him.

And in that moment, when my inhibitions were low and Parker had drowned out my every fear, I let myself fall completely apart, and even though he fell with me, he kept me wrapped in his arms holding our bodies pressed against one another. I didn't need some grand gesture like the romance novels that lined Staci's shelves because Parker James was all I had ever wanted love to be.

CHAPTER 32

HER BROTHER'S BEST FRIEND

PARKER

PRESENT

WHEN I KNOCKED on Mason's door, he opened it like I was crazy.

"Why did you knock? It wasn't locked was it?"

I walked in the door behind him. "Umm, no." *Why the fuck did I knock on the door?*

He pulled two beers out of the fridge, and I sat down at his kitchen bar. Livy was in the house somewhere. I knew because I dropped her off here earlier this morning. His house was filled with the scent of her, and I wanted nothing more than for that smell to linger in my home every day.

"What the fuck happened the other day? I wish you could have been there to see Emily's face when she realized you weren't coming. I thought she had been possessed." He chuckled and handed me one of the beers.

"Yeah." I laughed with him. "Our talk wasn't the most pleasant thing in the world."

"I'd say."

We sat in awkward silence for a moment, something that

never happened with us, and suddenly I felt like I was in high school again. I wasn't exactly sure how to tell one of my oldest best friends that I was insanely in love with his sister.

"Mason, I..." I took a deep breath.

"How did she react when you told her you were in love with Livy?"

My eyes jumped to his, and he had a large smirk on his face.

"Do you two think I'm stupid?" He crossed his arms.

"How long have you known?" I took a drink of my beer.

"Oh Lord." He ran his hand through his hair. "Probably since we were sixteen. You always wanted to hang out at the house when she was there, and you always pushed me to let her hang out with us."

"Huh." I chuckled. "I guess I never really did get it past you then."

"Not a chance." He looked down the hall toward his bedrooms. "You know you could have just told me though, right?"

"I know." I nodded. "I was just worried."

"We're best friends, Parker. Nothing will change that. Unless you hurt her again, of course. Then I'm going to have to kick your ass." He pointed his beer at me to prove his point.

"I won't hurt her." I stared him in the eyes to let him know I was serious, "But if on some off chance that I do, then I'll let you try."

"Yeah, right." He laughed before yelling Livy's name.

She came down the hall a moment later dressed in a pair of yoga pants and a tank top. I hadn't told her that I was coming here because I knew she would want to tell Mason together, but Mason was my best friend, and it was something we had to do alone.

She was lifting her hair in her hands as she made her way

into the kitchen, wrapping it in a knot on top of her head, and she stopped in her tracks when she saw me.

"Oh. Hey, Parker." She turned her back to me and grabbed a water out of the fridge.

"Hey."

Mason winked at me with a shit-eating grin on his face.

"Livy, do you have any plans tonight?"

"No." She leaned against the counter and all I could think about was all the things I had done to her on Staci's kitchen counter. "Why? What's up?"

"Well your boyfriend here," he waved his hand out to me and Livy choked on her water, "was just asking for my permission to take you on a date tonight."

I rolled my eyes at him, but Livy's mouth was wide open.

"You told him?" Her eyes bounced back and forth between her brother and me.

"He didn't tell me that you two were official now, but you just confirmed it." He smirked at his sister.

"I didn't say that." Her gaze flew to me then back to her brother. "We're just... we're just hanging out," she stammered.

"We're official." I took another sip of my beer.

"Parker!" She turned back toward me clearly uncomfortable with having this talk in front of her brother.

"What, babe? It's the truth. You're mine." I shrugged my shoulders. It was the truth, and it was simple.

"You don't get to just tell me that I'm yours." She crossed her arms over her chest, which caused her breasts to look amazing.

"I just did."

"You are such a caveman," she huffed.

"I'm pretty sure you told me once that you swoon when I act all territorial over you." I smiled, but she didn't.

"Oh, young love." Mason wrapped his arm around his

sister. “All that I ask is that you take your makeup sex to Parker’s house. I can deal with the two of you dating, but I can’t deal with having to listen to it.” He placed a kiss on Livy’s head before he disappeared into the back of the house.

LIVY

PRESENT

"I can't believe you still have this place. It looks amazing." I looked around the property of his house, a house that once belonged to his grandparents, and a place that held so many memories.

"Yeah. Papa left it to me when he passed. I've been slowly working on getting it in better shape."

The house was the same crisp white that I remembered, but instead of chipping paint, the years of wear had been sanded off and repainted. The flowerbeds that were completely overgrown the last time I was here were now cleared out and lined with rows and rows of flowers.

"I'm sorry I wasn't here." I looked up at him, and he was watching me. "For Papa. I loved him so much. You know?"

"He knew." He pulled me closer to him. "And he loved you too."

I nodded my head as I swallowed down my emotions.

"You should have heard him when you left." Parker chuckled. "I don't think I've ever heard him yell at me like that."

"Ouch." I grinned.

"Yeah. He told me that I was the biggest idiot he had ever met."

We were walking the edge of the small river that ran along the property line, and as I watched the water ripple over the rocks, I couldn't help but laugh.

"Papa was a pretty smart man."

Before I even realized what was happening, Parker swooped me up in his arms and held me over the water.

"Parker!"

"Are you saying that you agree with him?" He was grinning, a huge fucking grin, and I loved it.

I gripped my arms tightly around his neck. "I'm not saying that I don't."

I squealed as he pretended to drop me in the water and I held on tighter.

"Do not drop me in this water, Parker James. It's probably freezing."

"Oh, I'm sure it is, but you are going to have to do better than that."

"What do you want?" I begged while laughing uncontrollably.

"First, you can tell me how wonderful I am." He thought about it for a moment. "Then we'll go from there."

"Not happening."

He swooped down, the tips of my hair running through the water and splashing against my back.

"Oh my God! That's freezing!"

He smiled down at me. "I'm waiting."

"Fine." I huffed. "Parker, you are wonderful."

He shook his head. "Details, woman. Details."

I couldn't stop my laughter. "Well, you're really good at tattooing." I tapped my chin. "You're also really nice to look at."

He rolled his eyes.

"What about my bedroom skills?" His dimple popped out, and I wanted to trace it with my tongue.

"Well... I've only had a test drive really. You know how easily things can go wrong with the motor as soon as you get it home."

He growled and dropped me down into the water. I squealed as the water engulfed me, the cold water a shock to my skin. He laughed as he tried to move away from me, but I grabbed his leg causing him to trip and fall into the water beside me.

The splash of water hit me in the face, and I wiped my eyes to get rid of the river water and the tears.

"I can't believe you did that." He splashed more water at me as he moved his body over mine.

"You did it first! There was no way I was going in here alone."

He searched my face as I tried to control my laughter. I couldn't remember a time when I had felt this happy.

He brushed my hair out of my face before gripping my chin in his hand.

"You are so fucking beautiful."

He leaned up brushing his lips against mine, and I no longer cared about the ice-cold water that surrounded me. As soon as his lips touched mine, I got lost in him.

He stood up, his white t-shirt completely see-through and showing off the ink that covered his abs. I watched him as he moved, his jeans stuck to his legs, his hair in disarray.

He leaned down and gripped me in his arms like I weighed nothing. I wrapped my legs around his waist and stared at him. He was devastatingly handsome. His green eyes bright, his jaw sharp. I traced my finger over his full lips before he bit down on my fingertip. I groaned as his mouth closed around my finger, and he started moving us back toward the house.

I pressed my lips against his neck and licked the river water from his skin. His arms tightened around me, and I bit down on him. I could feel him at my center every time he walked, and when he finally slammed my back against the house, I was a writhing mess.

Using his hips to pin me against the siding, he ripped my shirt over my head and unhooked my bra. As the straps fell down my arms, I knew I should have been thinking about his neighbors catching us, but they were far enough away and frankly, I didn't give a damn.

"Remind me to thank, Staci." He mumbled against my skin as he traced the curve of my breast with his tongue.

"For what?" I looked down at him, watching him feast on my skin, and there was not a more beautiful sight in the world.

"These." He flicked his tongue against my nipple ring as his hand gently squeezed the other.

I threw my head back against the house, the sensation almost too much to bear.

He dropped me to my feet, before he fell to his knees, and ripped my yoga pants from my legs.

He didn't give me a moment to catch my breath before he placed my leg over his shoulder and his mouth against my pussy. I barely managed to hold my own weight as my leg began to shake under his assault, and he could tell too. He ran his hand slowly down my trembling leg, and when he reached my knee he pulled it over his shoulder as well.

My shoulders pressed into the house, my weight was supported by his shoulders, and sanity was slowly slipping away with each flick of his tongue.

I gripped my fingers in his wet hair, and I screamed out his name when he sucked my clit into his mouth. I was falling hard.

My legs clenched around his head as my orgasm rushed

through my body. My head slammed against the house, and my nails dug into my thighs.

I was on fire.

He continued to press soft kisses against me, and he slowly made his way up my body as he put each of my feet back to the ground.

His tongue ran against my neck and an aftershock of pleasure ran through my body.

"I need you in my bed," he whispered in my ear before gently sucking my earlobe into his mouth.

I nodded my head because I didn't trust my voice, and he lifted me up again, pushing the door open and walking into the house.

I tried to take in the home around me as he stormed through it, but his tongue was pressed against my neck and my body was pressed against his still wet clothing. Lust was coursing through my veins, and the only thing I could think about was how badly I needed him.

We crashed into a small table when I pressed my mouth against his, and I faintly heard something crash to the ground. I tugged at Parker's shirt, trying my hardest to pull it over his head. The fabric clung to his skin, but eventually, I managed to get it off. I laid my hands against his chest as he started making his way up the stairs. I ran my tongue over the date tattooed on his chest, and he tripped slightly, almost knocking us over.

He pressed my back against the wall, and he kissed me. A desperate fucking kiss. I could feel every bit of myself being taken by him with ever second that passed. I couldn't breathe with his mouth against mine, but he breathed for me. I couldn't think, but I didn't need to when he controlled my body so easily.

He kicked his bedroom door open when we finally made it

to the top of the stairs, and he threw me down on the bed with a bounce.

I sat up on my elbows watching him as he pulled his jeans and underwear from his legs. I squirmed as he made his way over to me, and I squealed when he gripped my ankle and jerked me to the end of the bed in one quick motion.

He looked down at me, his eyes on fire. "What do you want, Livy?"

There were so many things that I wanted in that moment, but as I looked up at his incredible body, there was only one thing that was on my mind.

"I want you in my mouth."

He groaned, his dick jumping at my words, and as he leaned his head back trying to control himself, I gripped him in my hands and got to my knees in front of him.

His skin was so smooth under my touch. I ran my fingers down the length of him before I pressed my lips to the tip of him. His hand gripped my hair, a bite of pain that only seemed to turn me on more, and I stared up into his eyes when his cock pressed past my lips and into my mouth.

He watched me, he fucking watched me like he never wanted to see anything else, and I felt myself become wetter under his gaze.

I circled my tongue around his tip before taking him as deep as I could. When he hit the back of my throat, his thighs shook under my hands.

His hands tightened in my hair as I hollowed out my cheeks, and he thrust into my mouth, his control gone.

I let him fuck my mouth, and I ate up every groan and every tremble. When he pulled out of my mouth, he put his hands under my arms and lifted me until I was facing him.

His hand tightened around my neck, and he forcefully pulled me against him, his mouth bruising my lips.

He lifted me in the air, my legs instantly going around his waist, and he pressed my back against the wall as he thrust into me.

I gripped his shoulders in my hands as he slammed his hips into mine. His touch was almost punishing, but I ate it up. I needed it. I wanted it. Harder, faster.

He bit down on my collarbone, and I felt myself tighten around him. His hands were gripping my ass and his eyes were watching where he slammed into me.

"God, Livy." His voice was breathless. "I will never get enough of you."

"I hope not." I chuckled but stopped the moment his tongue flicked against my nipple.

"Tell me you love me," he demanded while looking straight in my eyes.

"I love you, Parker."

He slammed into me again, and I fell apart around him.

"Fuck."

I was spiraling.

"Parker."

I couldn't see anything past him.

"Oh God."

He gripped my thigh in his hand lifting it against my chest, and he thrust into me until he fell over the edge with me.

Our bodies were covered in sweat and river water, and I never wanted to come down from the high.

I would take being bad with Parker James a million times over being good with anyone else.

CHAPTER 33

SHE NEEDED HIM

LIVY

PRESENT

I TRACED the ink over his side, and his skin broke out in goosebumps under my touch.

"What's this one?" I pointed to the red rose that stood out against so much black ink.

"That one is for my grandmother. Roses were her favorite."

I pressed a kiss against the rose then ran my hand over the portrait he had drawn of me that rested on his side.

"When did you get this?" I traced the lines that came out of the side of my face. It was a beautiful madness.

"About two years ago." He looked down at the tattoo and watched my fingers.

Two years ago.

Two years after I left.

I pressed my body against his and kissed the edge of his jaw.

"What was that for?" He was looking down at me and he looked so open and so vulnerable, and I never wanted that moment to end.

"For loving me."

He gripped my chin in his hand and pressed a kiss to my lips. "I couldn't stop loving you if I tried. And trust me. I did." He laughed before dipping his tongue into my mouth.

His phone rang, echoing through the room, but he didn't move his mouth from mine. His arms were wrapped around me, and I was completely wrapped up in him.

He kissed down my neck and my chest heaved under his touch. His phone rang again, but he continued to make his way down my body.

"Do you think you should get that?" I arched my body while he bit down against my ribs.

"If it's important, they'll call back."

His phone stopped ringing and immediately started ringing again.

"Fuck." He pulled his lips from my body then made his way across the room to grab his phone. I watched his ass as he walked away from me. His body was out of this world, and I wanted to trace every ridge and curve with my tongue.

"Hello?" He ran his hand through his hair and winked at me when he caught me checking him out.

I smiled and pulled his comforter up against my chest.

"What?" His voice sounded panicked, and I sat up in bed. "When?"

He pulled at the ends of his hair, and I stopped breathing.

"Okay. Yeah. Yeah. I'll be there." He pressed the end button on his phone, and I watched his back muscles bunch as he took a deep breath before turning to me.

"Livy, it's... It's Emily." He hesitated when he said her name, but I could see the desperation in his eyes. "She's been in a wreck. I... Fuck. I..."

"Go, Parker."

His eyes jumped to mine. "She still has me listed as her

emergency contact everywhere. That was the hospital. I need to call her family. I..."

"Parker..." I sat up on my knees and gripped his hands in mine. "She needs you. Go."

He searched my eyes before he gripped my neck and pulled me against him. He kissed my mouth desperately, and I tried to not let panic take over.

"I love you. You know that, right?"

"I know," I whispered against his mouth.

He pressed his forehead against mine then he let me go and started throwing on clothes. I climbed out of his bed and looked around his room for my clothes before I remembered that they were still outside.

"What are you doing?" He buttoned his jeans and lifted a t-shirt over his head.

"Getting dressed." I shrugged my shoulders as I stood in the center of his room completely naked.

"Please don't leave." He gripped my hands in his. "Stay here. I'll be back as soon as I can. I need to know that you're still here."

"I'll be here."

He pressed another kiss against my lips then he walked out the door to her.

CHAPTER 34

WHERE GOOD GIRLS GO TO DIE

PARKER

PRESENT

I WAS NOT PREPARED for walking into Emily's room. All the nurse had told me on the phone was that she had been in a car wreck. She didn't tell me any more details. She didn't tell me what kind of condition she was in.

She was connected to so many wires and tubes that I couldn't count them all. Bruises were already forming on her skin and there were bandages covering so many places.

"Are you Mr. James?" A voice called from behind me, and I turned to find a short nurse dressed in a pair of dark blue scrubs.

"Yes." I cleared my dry throat. "Yes. That's me."

She nodded her head before making her way around Emily's bed and checking the machines that were connected to her.

"Is she okay?" I looked around the room. There was a dry erase board on the wall that said the nurse's name, Amanda, and under Goals, there was nothing listed.

"It's quite early to know what all damage has been done,

but yes, your wife should be okay." She pressed a button on some machine that was pumping medicine into Emily.

"She's not my wife. She's my... She's my ex."

The nurse's eyes got big but she quickly recovered with a smile.

"I'm sorry. I just assumed since she asked for you."

"She asked for me?" My chest tightened at her words. Emily and I didn't work out, but that didn't mean that I didn't love her once.

"Yes. She was very intoxicated when the ambulance brought her in, but she was demanding for you. Your name was just about the only information the emergency room could get out of her." She straightened the blanket that lay over Emily as she talked.

"She was drinking and driving?" That didn't sound like Emily. She would never do something so reckless.

"Yes. She completely totaled her vehicle, but she was the only one involved. Thank God."

I ran my fingers through my hair and looked at Emily. She looked so fragile lying in that hospital bed. So... broken.

"She should wake up soon. I gave her some pain medicine a few hours ago that made her really sleepy."

I nodded my head as the nurse spoke.

Why would she drink and drive? What would make her be so reckless? Then it hit me.

Me.

Guilt flooded me, and I tried to pay attention as the nurse continued to talk about concussions and cuts.

She would have never done something like this before. Before I cancelled our wedding and broke her fucking heart.

"I need to call her family." I sat down next to Emily and ran my hand over hers.

"Okay. I'll give you some time alone." The nurse shut the

door behind her, and I felt like I was suffocating. I wished I was still at home in bed with Livy, but just that thought ate me alive with guilt.

Livy was right about me from the beginning, I fucked everything up. I've had two girls that truly loved me in this life, and I broke them both.

Neither one of them deserved it. Neither one of them should have ever been with me to start with because I was where good girls go to die.

CHAPTER 35

GUILT

LIVY

PRESENT

PARKER HAD BEEN GONE for five hours.

I knew five hours was nothing.

But I hadn't heard from him. Not one call or a text, and I'd be lying if I said that my chest wasn't tight with panic.

I sent him a text to let him know that I was here if he needed anything, but he hadn't replied.

I pathetically watched the screen to see those three little dots that meant he was typing, but they never came.

I was wearing nothing but one of his t-shirts. My clothes were in the washer. Even if I wanted to leave. I couldn't.

But I wouldn't.

I had run from him before, but I wouldn't let my fear win again.

But I couldn't stop my imagination from running wild. What was he doing? Was he comforting her? Was he thinking that he had made a mistake by choosing me over her?

Had he?

I sat down on his couch with a cup of hot chocolate in my

hand and stared out to the back porch where I had fallen apart under his touch yesterday.

When everything was perfect.

I curled up in a blanket and watched a movie. When I still hadn't heard from Parker two hours later, I became even more worried.

I pressed his name with a trembling finger and held the phone to my ear. When I heard his voice through the other end of the phone, I finally breathed.

"Livy."

"Parker, is everything okay?" I tucked my knees into my chest.

He took a deep breath and I heard it through the phone. "She's beat up pretty badly. She has a concussion, and she had to have six stitches in her forehead."

I could hear how worried he was through the phone.

"What happened?"

"She was drinking and driving," he said softly.

"Wow."

"She was... She was drinking because of me. We would have been on our honeymoon right now, Livy."

"Don't do that, Parker."

"Do what?" He sounded frustrated.

"Do not blame yourself for this happening to her." His guilt was so tangible that even I could feel it, but it was misplaced. "She made the choice to get behind the wheel of her car. Not you."

"I need to go. Her parents are just now getting here."

"Okay." I nodded my head even though he couldn't see it. "I'm not leaving, Parker."

He was silent, and that silence scared me far more than his words.

"I love you."
"I love you too, Livy."

CHAPTER 36

YOU LOVE HER MORE

PARKER

PRESENT

"PARKER." She reached out for me.

"Hey, Emily." I sat down beside her hospital bed.

"What happened?" She looked around the room, confused.

"You were in a car accident. Do you not remember?"

She blinked her eyes, her face black and blue from the wreck.

"I remember going out drinking with the girls. I remember." She stopped and looked at me. "I was drunk."

I nodded my head, and she closed her eyes.

"I'm such an idiot."

I didn't say anything because she was right. Drinking and driving was idiotic. She didn't need me yelling at her for her to realize that.

"Where are my parents?" She looked toward the door.

"They went downstairs to get some lunch. I told them I would stay here in case you woke up."

She looked up at me, so much hope in her eyes. "Why are you here, Parker?"

"They said you kept saying my name over and over when they brought you in."

She tried to bring her hand up to her face, but all the cords and tubes stopped her.

"I'm sorry, Parker. That's so embarrassing." She chuckled, but it was completely fake.

"I'm the one who is sorry, Emily. I never meant for things to be like this. I never wanted to hurt you."

"I know." She leaned her head back against her pillow. "But it still hurts."

I nodded my head. I didn't know what I could say to her to make it better. I didn't know if there was anything I could say.

"Is she worth it?" She was staring at me, and as much as I didn't want to hurt her more, I couldn't lie to her.

"I'm in love with her, Emily. I have been since I was sixteen years old."

She bit her lip and I could see tears forming in her eyes. "Did you love me?"

My chest ached because I did love her. I didn't love her in the way that I loved Livy, but it didn't mean that our love hadn't meant something.

"I did."

"But you love her more."

I didn't answer her. I just looked at her, and she nodded her head. She already knew the answer.

"Why are you here, Parker?"

"I already told you. You kept saying my name and..."

"No, Parker." She shook her head.

"Why are you here?"

I stared at her, the girl that I almost married, and the guilt ate me up inside. "I feel so guilty, Emily. I just... I want you to be happy. I walked in here, and I saw you like this." I motioned toward her. "You wouldn't be here if it wasn't for me."

"Stop." She put her hand on top of mine. "I would give anything to have you still. Anything." She took a deep, trembling breath. "But I don't want to spend my life with someone who's in love with someone else. I deserve better than that."

"I know you do." Emily deserved everything good. She deserved the world.

"Don't waste it. We broke up because you're in love with her. Don't make her question that."

Her words hit me hard in the chest.

"Go to her."

I stood up, kissing Emily on the forehead, kissing her for the last time. "Thank you."

I walked to the door, but Emily called my name as I turned the handle.

"I don't blame you, you know? You can't help who you love."

And with her forgiveness, my heart broke a little more because I didn't deserve it.

CHAPTER 37

HE NEEDED ME

LIVY

PRESENT

WHEN PARKER finally walked in the door, I could feel the darkness that surrounded him.

He set his keys down on the counter and stared at me from across the room.

"You're still here." His voice was soft and just hearing it seemed to calm some of my anxiety.

"I told you I would be."

He nodded his head, but I could see how lost he was in his eyes.

"Are you okay?"

He shook his head and looked away from me.

"I'm just tired. I'm going to jump in the shower. Okay?"

I nodded my head and he made his way up the stairs without a backward glance.

As I watched his back disappear up the stairs, my chest ached. He was hurting. It was clear to see it, but I didn't know how to make it better. I didn't know how to make him let me back in.

I walked up the stairs and I heard the shower kick on as I

entered his room. He had left the door cracked open, and even though I knew I was invading his privacy, I stood at the door and watched him. His forehead pressed against the shower wall, the cascade of water raining down on him.

I stripped my clothes off until I was completely bare, and I stepped into the shower behind him. He didn't lift his head when he heard the shower door, but I watched the muscles of his back tense.

"Livy, what are you doing?"

"Parker, please." I ran my hands down his back before pressing my chest against him.

"I'm sorry, Livy. I'm just fucked up in my head right now. I just need... I don't know. I need to be alone."

"Let me help you," I whispered before I pressed my lips against his back.

He shook his head, water flying around him. "I'm just so mad at myself. I'm so fucking angry." He slammed his fist against the shower wall, and I wrapped my arms around his chest.

"Take it out on me, Parker. Let me help you let go."

He turned toward me, finally looking me in the eyes. "I love you, Livy."

"I know," I nodded my head, "but fuck me like you don't."

He slammed my back into the shower wall, the cold tile hitting my back, and his body surrounding me.

His mouth met mine in a rush. His kiss was sloppy and wet and full of anger. He lifted me up, his fingers digging into my thighs before he lined his cock up with his hand and thrust inside me without warning.

He thrust into me hard and angry, and I moaned as he hit a spot inside of me that begged for more. I took all of him. His anger. His need. His possession.

Pressure built inside me that was far more powerful than

anything I had ever felt before. He bit down on my neck before he dropped me back down to my feet, and he spun me around. His hand was buried in my hair and my back was arched to the point of pain.

But he didn't stop.

He thrust into me from behind and my hands pressed against the wet tiles trying to find something to hold onto. He pulled on my hair turning my face toward his, and he kissed me while he slammed harder into my body.

He released my hair making my upper body jolt forward, and I gripped the edge of the shower as his fingers gripped my ass. He reached his hand around my body and just when I thought I couldn't take anymore, he slapped my clit with his hand and I screamed out his name as I came around him.

He thrust into me harder and my hands slipped, no longer strong enough to hold me. Parker caught my weight though and he carried me out of the shower and set me on the bathroom counter.

Shit fell to the floor as he pushed my body up on the granite, but neither one of us cared. He thrust into me again. Harder and harder, and even though I had just come, I felt it building inside me again.

His hand on my hip was bruising me and his mouth was punishing against my breast. He slammed into me, my back crashing into the mirror, and he watched me as he ripped the next orgasm from my body.

I screamed, this orgasm much more powerful than the last, and I felt like I had completely lost control. He pulled my hips closer to him as I rode out the waves of pleasure, and I felt his cock twitch inside me.

"You are mine, Livy."

"Yes," I called out, my voice rough with pleasure.

"Say it. I need to hear you fucking say it." He slammed into me again driving his point home.

"I'm yours, Parker."

He slammed into me, harder and harder, and he looked me straight in the eye. "I fucking love you, Livy."

I leaned up, sucking the water off his neck, and he groaned as he came inside me.

He wrapped his arms around me and pulled me so tightly into him that I could barely breathe, but I didn't need anything but him in that moment. And he needed me.

CHAPTER 38

GETTING STARTED

PARKER

PRESENT

I WOKE up with Livy fast asleep on my chest. As I watched her breathe, her small body lifted and falling against mine, I couldn't figure out how I had gotten so fucking lucky.

I had let the guilt I was feeling over Emily eat me up. It had taken over everything else, but Livy wouldn't let it.

She always knew exactly what I needed. She had always been exactly what I needed.

And I needed to be more for her.

I refused to waste any more time.

I rolled her over, her hair falling over the pillow, her body completely on display. I ran my hand down her side, and she squirmed in her sleep.

When I pressed my mouth against her pussy, she moaned and her back lifted off the bed. I ran my tongue over her softly, remembering how rough I was with her the night before, and she buried her hands in my hair before she ever opened her eyes.

"Good morning," she purred as I sucked her clit into my mouth.

"Mornin'," I said against her skin, causing her legs to tighten around my head.

She didn't say another word as I gripped her ass in my hands and pushed her further against my mouth. I pushed my finger into her tightness, curling it upwards, and making her legs shake around me.

She tried to clamp her legs closed when the pleasure became too much, but I spread her open with my hands and forced her to take what I was giving her.

She trembled under my touch and just when she was about to come, I stopped. She jerked her head up to look at me as I lay back on the bed beside her.

"What the fuck was that?" She looked a little crazy, and I loved knowing I was the one who was making her that way.

"Sit on my face, Livy."

I watched her eyes darken, and she didn't give it any thought before she moved over me and lowered her pussy to my lips.

I gripped her hips in my hands and forced her further down on my mouth, and her hands clasped onto the headboard while she stared down at me. I didn't move my gaze away from hers as I devoured her flesh.

She was so wet, and I fucking loved it. I loved the way she tasted, I loved the way her eyes clouded over in lust, and I loved the way she finally lost control when I sucked her clit into my mouth and started grinding against my face.

She was almost there. I could feel it and so could she. She grabbed her tits in her hands, a beautiful fucking sight, and I ran my teeth over her clit.

She wasn't expecting it, her body slamming harder against my mouth, and she screamed.

She screamed as she rode out her orgasm against my face.

She screamed as I pushed her pleasure further than she thought it could go by sucking her clit back into my mouth.

She fell to the bed beside me with a lazy smile on her lips.

I moved over her body kissing every inch of skin I could find.

“I’m so sleepy again,” she giggled as I kissed her hips.

“Well you better wake up, baby, because we’re just getting started.”

CHAPTER 39

THIS IS NOT A DRILL

LIVY

PRESENT

WE HAD BARELY LEFT the house in two days. It was two perfect days of sex, food, and nothing else.

By the time we finally surfaced into Forbidden Ink, Staci and Brandon stood at my desk clapping.

I tucked my face into Parker's side in embarrassment, and Parker only chuckled.

"Don't you two have work to do?" Parker set the coffees we had just bought on my desk.

"I don't know. Do we?" Brandon asked. "You two have been in your sex dungeon so long that we thought we might have to shut this place down."

"Shut up, Brandon." I shoved his shoulder as I walked around my desk.

"It's true," Staci said with her hands on her hips. "I thought I was going to have to find a new bestie."

She winked at me and I wrapped my arms around her.

"Wait, I thought I was your bestie," Brandon pouted beside me.

"I can have more than one bestie, Brandon."

He smiled until Staci poked her head over my shoulder. "But I'm the best bestie."

Staci and I laughed as Brandon tried to grab her, but she was too quick.

"How about we have a bestie night tonight since you both have been so neglected?" I asked, and Parker rolled his eyes.

"Yes!" Staci clapped her hands. "But you're getting ready with me. You've been spending too much time with Parker already."

I laughed but agreed and then we all got to work.

STACI and I had been at the karaoke bar for about fifteen minutes when Brandon finally walked in the door. It was the same karaoke bar that Parker took me on our first date, and even though we were having a bestie night, I couldn't help feeling even more in love with Parker for him suggesting that we come here.

"Where's Parker?" I asked Brandon over the loud singing.

He had texted me about ten minutes ago to tell me he was almost here.

"He'll be here in a sec," Brandon said before cheering for the guy doing a hardcore rendition of "Highway to Hell".

Staci and I had already put our name in to sing a Spice Girls' song, and we had each taken a few shot to help bring out our inner divas. We were both giggling at nothing when I said, "I love this song."

The guitar riff of "Sex on Fire" by Kings of Leon started blaring through the speakers of the bar, and I turned to see who had the balls to sing that song.

"Holy shit," Staci started laughing beside me, and I looked up on the stage to see Parker on the stage with the microphone in his hand.

But that wasn't what made me giggle. Parker was dressed in jeans, a white t-shirt with a bright yellow jacket over it, and a fireman hat. My grand gesture.

He started singing the lyrics, and the girls in the bar started going crazy. I didn't blame them. He looked hot as hell.

He pointed at our table as he sang the words, and I covered my face as Staci doubled over with laughter beside me.

He jumped off the stage, the microphone still in his hand, and made his way over to me. He pulled my stool toward him, and he spread my legs apart with his hands as he leaned into me. I couldn't stop laughing as he shimmied his body against me.

The crowd around us was cheering and cat calling as he sang and danced. He winked at me as he pulled off his fireman hat and placed it on my head. He pulled the jacket off his back, before swinging it in the air to the cheers from the crowd. He threw it to me, and I barely caught it against my chest because I was too busy watching the way he was circling his hips.

When the song ended, he dropped the mic to the ground, which the DJ frowned at, and he grabbed my face in his hands.

"You are insane." I was laughing so hard that I snorted which only made Parker smile harder.

"Most romance books are." He smirked. "And you needed a grand gesture."

"You are my grand gesture, Parker. You're all I need."

He gripped my thighs in his in hands and lifted me up. I wrapped my legs around his waist and everyone cheered again. I buried my face in his neck, embarrassed by all the attention, and laughed as he carried me toward the back of the bar.

"What are we doing?" I looked behind me as he turned the lock on an office door. "We're not allowed to be in here," I whispered like we were going to get caught.

"Shhh..." he said against my lips as he set me down on the desk, and I laughed again.

"No way, Parker James. We are not doing this."

I looked back at the door, but it was still securely locked.

"Baby, are you scared?" he teased as he ran his hands down my body.

"I'm not scared." My blood was rushing through my veins thinking about us getting caught at any second, but I wouldn't dare admit that to him.

He pushed my legs apart and ran his hands down my jean-clad legs.

"Then show me what kind of bad girl you can be." He grinned a devilish grin, and I felt lost in my draw to him.

I pushed him off me and onto the desk chair that sat behind him before I slowly pulled my shirt up my stomach and over my head.

He watched me as I rolled my hips to the music that could barely be heard in the secluded office, and his eyes clouded over in lust as I dropped to the floor in front of him on my knees.

I had danced in front of hundreds of men during my time at Toxic, and every time I had felt ashamed or dirty. But I had never felt like this. I had never felt so wanted or so loved. I looked up into Parker's eyes as I rolled my body against him, and he groaned when my ass pressed into his lap.

"Tell me what you want, Parker," I purred as I ran my fingers down his thighs.

"You. It's always been you."

I turned to face him, straddling his hips. "You've got me."

"I love you," he murmured against my lips.

"I love you too."

He pushed my hair out of my face. "I've always loved you. Even when you were gone, I always woke up looking for you. I searched for you subconsciously even when I told myself I shouldn't." He shook his head and a tear ran down my cheek.

"But love is a word that is too weak and used too often to describe what I feel for you. It's relentless and desperate, and every time you smile I fall harder and harder."

"Parker," I whispered his name because I didn't know what else to say.

"Don't ever leave me again, Livy." He clung to me, my body pressed desperately tight against his.

"Never."

THE END

OTHER BOOKS BY HOLLY RENEE:

I hope you enjoyed Where Good Girls Go to Die with Livy and Parker! If you want more from their world, keep reading for the synopsis of Staci's and Brandon's stories, Where Bad Girls Go to Fall and Where Bad Boys are Ruined.

WHERE BAD GIRLS GO TO FALL

THE GOOD GIRLS SERIES, BOOK 2

A Best Friend's Brother Romance

Nothing good came from listening to my heart.

It was careless and irrational and became way too invested when I read a romance novel.

So I put her under lock and key.

I only had a few rules, and I always stuck with them.

1. Never get attached.

2. Always run before the feels become contagious.

3. No matter what, under no circumstances, never fall in love.

He was a playboy who ran by the same set of rules.

What we had together was fun, it was hot, and it was temporary.

Until he screwed everything up.

We were never meant to be each other's happily ever after, but the harder I tried to push him away, the further I fell.

WHERE BAD BOYS ARE RUINED

THE GOOD GIRLS SERIES, BOOK 3

A Good Girl/ Bad Boy Romance

I ate leftover cupcakes and cracked macarons for breakfast.

I was ninety percent sure he simply ate up girls like me.

I was covered in paint splatters, cake batter, and sweat the first time I met him.

He was covered in badass tattoos and a smile that seemed to hold a secret I would never figure out.

Rule number 1 was never, under any circumstances, fall for the man who I wrote my lease check to.

So, I tucked him away in the "Fantasize Only" compartment of my brain and called it a day.

But he didn't make it easy.

He was arrogant, funny, and the biggest flirt I had ever met.

Most of the time, I didn't know if I was just a game to him.

If I didn't know better, I'd say he was on a mission to ruin my life.

And maybe my heart, too.

THE WRONG PRINCE CHARMING

A College Romance

EVERY LITTLE GIRL dreams of being swept off her feet by a charming Prince.

But my life was no fairy tale.

And in this kingdom called college, the rules went out the window.

I'd known golden boy, Theo Hunt, was the one for me since we were kids. My heart was his for the taking, but I had become nothing more than the MVP of the campus king's friend-zone.

Easton Cole was a storm I couldn't have predicted. He knocked me off my feet and stole my heart. But he was off limits. Not only was he was Theo's frat brother, but he was the teacher's assistant in English 101 and I was acing every test.

My heart was torn, my feelings tangled.

Because as soon as I noticed Easton, Theo finally noticed me.

I was in love with two guys, as different as night and day, but I could only have one.

I only hoped I didn't choose The Wrong Prince Charming.

BOTTOMS UP

THE ROCK BOTTOM SERIES, BOOK 1

A Friends to Lovers Romance

From the moment I met him, I knew he was trouble.

He was reckless, cocky, and everything I shouldn't want.

I had a life all figured out, and Tucker Moore was not a part of the plan.

But somehow I slipped.

One moment I had it all under control.

The next I was spiraling around him, begging him for whatever he would give me.

But as quickly as I fell for him, it all crumbled around us.

Because everything I thought I knew was far from the truth.

There was only one way to fix what we had done.

So I turned my world Bottoms Up.

DOUBLE SHOT

A Sexy Office Romance

HOW DO you screw up your life in three steps? Easy.

Step one: Graduate from college with no prospective jobs lined up.

Step two: Move back home with your parents because no job unfortunately equals no money.

Step three: Forget to Facebook stalk the guy who broke your heart before accepting a job in a town that has a smaller population than a frat party on a Wednesday night.

I could quit but living with my parents forever didn't seem like a solid life plan.

Jase Hale was the golden boy. Our boss thought he was beyond talented. The receptionist sent him more flirty smiles and baked goods than was considered normal for a woman old enough to be his mom.

I tried to avoid him and his undeniable charm at all costs.

He did everything he could to get under my skin.

Every encounter left me reeling.

Every smirk made my stomach flip.

I assumed he was playing with me, just pushing my buttons like always, but when he lifted me onto my desk and shut me up with his lips on mine, I was more confused than ever.

It didn't matter that he was trying to prove me wrong. Having my heart broken by the same jerk twice in one lifetime wasn't an option.

He only got one shot with me and he sure as hell didn't order a double.

STAY UP TO DATE ON FUTURE RELEASES!

Click this link to sign up for the Holly Renee Mailing List:
Newsletter

Stay connected with Holly Renee:

Facebook

Instagram

ACKNOWLEDGMENTS

Thank you to all the readers that have taken a chance on my book. I know that there are so many books to choose from, and I can't tell you what it means to me that you decided to spend your time with mine. It means the fucking world.

Thank you to every single blogger who has taken the time to share, read, and review my book. This book world would be absolutely nothing without you! You are the unicorns. Don't forget it. I am forever indebted to you.

To my husband, thank you once again for supporting my crazy ideas and allowing me to do what I love even though it's not always the most convenient. I wouldn't survive this world without you having my back. You are my biggest cheerleader, and I love you more that you can imagine.

Thank you, thank you, thank you to Cheryl Lucero for hanging with me for every single step of the way! Your feedback and encouragement have been amazing, and I couldn't have done this without you!

Thank you to my bestie and my mom for reading this book in the smallest segments with the biggest cliff hangers! Thank you for begging me for more and keeping my ass going.

Thank you to Dustin Lane Collins for spending hours and hours drawing the beautiful artwork that is featured in the book. I love you to pieces. *Jackhammer* ;)

Thank you to Ellie McLove, Regina Wamba, and Shari Ryan for being a part of this project! All three of you are insanely talented, and I can't thank you enough for helping my vision come to life.

xo, Holly

Made in the USA
Middletown, DE
17 September 2021